MONTANA SKIES

Bored with civilian life following the end of the Civil War, three former Union soldiers — brothers Jeff and Clem Jackson, and their cousin Dan — move to a family ranch in the Yellowstone Valley, Montana. But much of the area is controlled by ruthless Scottish rancher Alexander Brown, whose gunmen enforce his determination to be the biggest business in the territory. With the sheriff also in Brown's pay, the Jacksons must fight back. But who will win the inevitable showdown?

JAKE SHIPLEY

MONTANA SKIES

Complete and Unabridged

LINFORD
Leicester

First published in Great Britain in 2013 by
Robert Hale Limited
London

First Linford Edition
published 2015
by arrangement with
Robert Hale Limited
London

A catalogue record for this book is available
from the British Library.

ISBN 978–1–4448–2575–6

Published by
F.A. Thorpe (Publishing)
Anstey, Leicestershire

Set by Words & Graphics Ltd.
Anstey, Leicestershire
Printed and bound in Great Britain by
T.J. International Ltd., Padstow, Cornwall

This book is printed on acid-free paper

1

Appomattox, Virginia. 8 April 1865
Captain Jeff Jackson led his weary
column down the gentle slope of a dirt
lane pitted with the tracks of heavy
wagons. It hadn't rained for two nights
but the ground was still slippery-damp
for even the surest-footed horse.

Jeff looked back at his men. The
fresh-faced bugler smiled, the men at
the front of the column were dozing as
they rode. After three days in the saddle
the troop was near to exhaustion.

A stone pinged noisily away from
Atlas's hoofs, slamming into a tree
trunk with a loud smack a moment
before Jeff saw the welcoming glow of
campfires.

A bleary-eyed commissary sergeant
waved a flaming torch to direct the
newcomers to the bivouac area.

Jeff raised a tired arm to halt the

troop then gave the order to dismount and set up camp, wondering what new part of hell he had led his men into.

The ravaged landscape was littered with the signs of a fierce battle. Blackened stumps of trees stood in silent vigil — a ghastly memorial to the dead and dying.

Jeff swung down from Atlas's back; a corporal wrangler caught the bridle.

'I'll look after him, Cap'n.' The soldier led the big black away.

Jeff looked around mournfully. A new campsite, no doubt as uncomfortable as any he had seen in the past four years, and with it the prospect of another battle.

★ ★ ★

Still tired next morning, Jeff rubbed his aching eyes. The little sleep he'd had hadn't come easy. He yawned and stretched his aching legs before stamping his big feet into his boots. He fastened on his sword and pistol belt and lifted the stained flap of the tent, accepting a tin cup of bitter coffee laced with acorns.

The first tell-tale sounds of Confederate troops forming up pierced the uneasy silence. The metallic rattle of sabres and ordnance drifted across the misty valley separating the two armies.

Daylight blossomed, colouring the ravaged land with an eerie yellow light. No birds ventured forth on this chill morning with its frosty air crisp on Jeff's lips and cheeks, the hairs inside his nose stiff and prickly.

The red earth was bone hard. Stones, freezing cold, mirrors of frost on their upper surfaces. An icy wind dug deep into arms and legs, reddening faces and hands already filled with tension.

Jeff stretched his back to relieve the stiffness as a sudden gust whipped through the stoic ranks. Pennants and flags fluttered wildly, amplifying the sound of taut material that cracked like a collection of bullwhips. He scanned the gaunt faces of his troop, each filled with its own expression, distinctive, but somehow the same.

Deep in his heart, Jeff longed to be far away from this place of death. To mount his horse and gallop away. He wondered where Atlas was right now. He hadn't seen the horse since the corporal wrangler had taken him away; hopefully he was enjoying a bag of oats fed by his cousin, Sergeant Dan Jackson, and his band of farriers. Atlas was the fourth horse Jeff had ridden since the start of the war; the other three had died of their wounds, or — more correctly — had been put out of their misery.

'Jeff.' Jeff felt the heavy nudge on his shoulder and turned. 'Breakfast.'

Sergeant Clem Jackson set down a chunk of flat wood; the makeshift plate contained four fried eggs and a slab of black bread.

Jeff's eyes widened with anticipated pleasure. 'Where did you get those?' he asked his younger brother.

'Don't ask,' Clem grinned. 'What the

eye don't see . . . ' Clem tapped his nose and winked. 'Let's just say the major won't be dining this good on this fine spring morning. Best eat 'em quick.'

Jeff crammed a chunk of bread into his mouth behind a slice of egg.

'Good, eh?' Clem scraped up the last bit of yolk with a piece of bread, shoving it into his mouth with a contented grunt. He ran his sleeve across his whiskered chin, pointing to a tiny piece of egg that had lodged itself in his brother's luxuriant beard.

Jeff brushed away the egg with the back of his hand.

The sound of boots scrambling on hard earth caused the brothers to turn.

A runner slid next to Jeff, saluting. 'Beggin' yer pardon, Captain. Colonel's compliments.' The messenger handed over a soiled scrap of paper. To Clem, the messenger repeated the salute, 'Sergeant.'

Clem nodded civilly.

Jeff unfolded the order, his face

showing no emotion as he read the words.

'Tell the colonel I understand.'

The messenger saluted, and scurried away.

'It appears we'll be making a push at eight o'clock. We're to wait at the end of that wall,' Jeff pointed, 'in that stand of cottonwoods. Come on, we got around forty minutes to get in position.'

Jeff and his men crouched low as they ran across the rear of the Union lines, heads tucked well down into collars, hoping the slim piece of cloth would protect them.

Inside the cottonwoods the grey-stone wall topped a steep rise above the enemy's left flank; a sunken lane ran across the crest. Alongside the wall a narrow water rill ran clear and inviting. Some took the opportunity to slake their sudden thirst; some dampened bandannas and wiped their faces and necks.

On the other side of the lane a broken-down picket fence marked the boundary of a rutted field.

Thirty minutes later, the big guns of the Union artillery opened up. The Confederate gunners soon responded. Cannonballs whistled through the air, before crashing down in a maelstrom of debris and bodies.

'Check your weapons,' Jeff ordered. His sergeants repeated his orders to those troopers out of earshot.

At eight o'clock, the centre of the Union line attacked, followed by a much bigger attack from the left. The din was calamitous as heavy artillery ordnance boomed out, shells exploding with disastrous consequences all along the Confederate line.

The two-pronged Union attack had the desired effect — pushing forward, bayonets fixed, mouths set in a steely grimace. The Confederate line broke, sprinting away from the cannon shells and the multitude of troops striding towards them in the only direction open to them — towards Jeff's unit. Up the steep slope they ran, each step more laboured as the incline took its toll on tired calves and thighs.

Jeff ordered his men to hold their fire until he gave the order, sweating hands on stocks and rifle barrels, fingers on steel-blue triggers that twitched and threatened to lock. The blue-coated Union soldiers watched the ragged grey line slowly edging closer. Faces became clearer. Blue uniforms were visible behind the wall. Rebel officers suddenly realized that a deadly welcome would soon greet them.

The ground ran red with Confederate blood, the smoke-charged air filled with the piercing screams of men, wounded and dying. Bodies jerked, guts spilled, inaudible shouts of surrender, unheard cries for mercy, but the hail of hot lead showed no sign of abating. Men fell one after the other as they tried to raise the Dixie flag in defiance of the Union troops who now stood in plain view, faces stained black with powder burns, arms feeling like they were about to fall off, lips sore, jaws aching.

Long before the firing ceased Jeff knew he would never forget the screams. A few sporadic musket balls whistled overhead, others smacked harmlessly into the wall, bullets of lead flattening before falling, spent, to the ground. Rebel officers tried to form men into a line to fight a rearguard, sabres flashed as they beat at the soldiers with the flat of their swords, horses whinnied and screamed a ghostly anthem.

Suddenly, among the dead and dying, despairing men were casting aside their weapons, throwing up their hands in surrender, their faces filled with horrific expressions. It was like shooting fish in a barrel — sickening. Still the firing continued, the land now covered by dirty-grey powder-filled smoke.

Not one rebel soldier made it out of that valley of death uninjured, caught as they were in a murderous crossfire.

Apart from sporadic gunfire somewhere over to the west the battlefield grew strangely silent. Men on both sides licked their wounds, drawing upon whatever reserves of strength they had left, knowing they had been lucky to have survived the carnage, and praying to God for safe deliverance in the next bout of fighting.

An hour or so before noon, truce flags being waved by the Confederates were clear to be seen; many guessed that the rebels wanted a temporary truce so that they could treat their wounded and carry away their dead. Then the news spread — the war was over. Lee had surrendered to Grant. The camp seemed to let out one huge sigh of relief.

The Appomattox battlefield was cleared of the dead and dying. General Lee's Confederates surrendered their weapons and headed for home, but for some units of the victorious Union army, life was not that simple. The government had been somewhat taken by surprise by Lee's capitulation and had no plan in place for decommissioning.

Along with a number of cavalry regiments, Jeff's unit was held back for a time as a precaution against further insurgency.

Word came of sporadic skirmishes in the west where pockets of Confederate resistance refused to accept the South's capitulation. Eventually Jeff received orders that his unit could proceed to their decommissioning point.

2

Evansville, Indiana

The dirt roads of Indiana proclaimed their homecoming, victors returning after vanquishing their foe. Tales of King Arthur and his knights returning to Camelot sprang into Jeff's mind — one of his favourite stories as a child — however, right now childhood seemed a very long time ago; it was the future that concerned him.

On the eve of that final battle Jeff had wrestled with the question of whether to return to teaching. Before the war his mind had been clear, he would accept the offer of a professorship in Boston. Now, though, his thoughts were a maelstrom of uncertainty. After the excitement of his recent life the notion of being stuck in a classroom had lost its earlier appeal. He resolved not to make any hasty decisions; he'd see how things went once he arrived home.

One thing was certain: there was no need to worry about money, for the time being at least — they had the security of their back-pay, plus the stash of Mexican silver dollars liberated from a Confederate paymaster.

On a ridge above the town of Evansville the three riders paused to take in a view they hadn't seen for four years. The wide Ohio River sparkled below to welcome them home.

'Home,' said Clem.

They dug in their spurs and suddenly they were there — home. The red-brick house, the white picket fence and gate — both looked freshly painted.

* * *

What followed was a welcome-home party to end all parties — everyone got wonderfully drunk and ate far too much.

Two weeks later the novelty of

peacetime had worn thin. The obligatory visits their mother had arranged had finally been exhausted. The time had come to reconstruct their lives, to blend back into society.

Clem returned to his old job at the riverboat terminal. Dan began work as a wagon driver at the general store owned by his mother's new beau. Jeff took longer to settle; he visited a couple of local schools and sat in on a few lessons, still unsure whether teaching was for him.

After much consideration Jeff wrote to the university in Boston to explain that he was unable to accept their offer of an English professorship. He did a little teaching, but became increasingly depressed. The horrors of war still appalled him, but, he reflected, he had to admit that living life on the edge had been seductive — excitement was a drug he missed more than he cared to admit.

Jeff rode Atlas most evenings, sometimes missing dinner. His mother sensed the restlessness in her eldest son. He loved being with his family again, but somehow he needed more, something that as yet he hadn't been able to put his finger on.

The thrilling feeling of the wind in his face whenever he galloped Atlas across the lush green countryside along the Ohio River somewhat anaesthetized the ache he felt inside. He realized how much being in the saddle meant; the thought of not to be able to ride whenever he wanted would surely kill him. Funny, he thought. Before the war, riding had never held the same fascination.

It wasn't long before Clem joined his brother, sometimes riding when he should have been at work; and when Dan got to hear about the equine activities of his two cousins he too joined in.

★ ★ ★

Jeff poked the fire with a stick. He looked at his brother's face glowing red in the firelight. 'Did I tell you I've decided against going to Boston?' Jeff poked the fire again. 'I'm not sure I can settle down to such a quiet life.'

Clem looked up, his face a picture of concentration.

Dan sprang up onto his haunches in a eureka moment. 'You boys as bored as I am?'

Clem and Jeff exchanged glances then looked at Dan; all three seemed to know what the others were thinking.

'Let's saddle up and head west,' Dan suggested out of the blue, 'catch us some wild horses, sell 'em to the army.'

Dan's excited words echoed what was in Jeff's heart, but before he could answer, Clem piped up enthusiastically, 'OK. Let's do it. When do we go?'

'Whoa. Hold on,' Jeff cautioned. Their faces were suddenly downcast. 'I'm not saying no, only that we need to take a little time to decide where to go and exactly what we plan to do when we get there.'

'Don't pour cold water over everything, Jeff. We don't need a plan, let's just saddle up and head west,' Clem chided, looking to Dan for support.

'Jeff's right,' Dan said. Clem looked unhappy. 'But,' Dan added, 'you're right as well. I say let's take a week to get everything sorted and then it's west for us.'

'Right,' Clem gushed, 'that's the when sorted, now the where.' Clem touched his brother's shoulder. 'Jeff, remember that cousin Pa used to tell us about? A rancher, farmer or something in Montana? We could head there.'

'Yeah!' Dan cried out enthusiastically. 'I remember.'

Jeff pondered the suggestion. He had to admit that the notion of life as a cowboy had an exciting appeal to it.

Clem wasn't about to let the grass grow under his feet. 'Let's talk to Pa about it as soon as we get back.'

He and Dan shook hands then turned to Jeff, two beaming faces, like the two little kids he had known all their lives, looking up to their natural leader. Jeff smiled and nodded.

'Whoopee!' shouted Dan.

* * *

'So, your minds are made up?' Pa Jackson asked sternly. 'Your ma ain't going to be happy, you know that, don't you?' His tone softened. 'I'll write to my cousin Jim in Montana, tell him you're coming. Haven't heard from him in years. Hopefully he won't mind you three scrag-ends paying him a visit. We used to write a lot, but, well I guess things slip when you get older. You'd better hope he still lives in the same place.' Joe called out to his wife. 'Any idea where Cousin Jim's letters are?'

Ma Jackson appeared from the kitchen, wiping her hands on a red and white cloth; she had flour on her nose and cheeks. 'Jim's letters?' A knowing expression lit up her eyes. 'Bureau,' she said, 'bottom drawer.'

She crossed the room and pulled out the bottom drawer of the big walnut bureau that stood proudly against one wall of the parlour, lifted the lid of a rosewood box and sifted through the contents. She selected three or four sheets of paper and held them towards her husband.

'These are the last ones he wrote, I guess.'

Joe put down the newspaper he'd been reading. 'Let's see 'em,' he said, holding out a hand.

'Don't you move a muscle, Joseph Jackson. I'm only baking bread as well as doing all the other chores around here. You just sit there, busy like, and I will bring the letters to you,' she scolded. 'Want me to read 'em for you as well?'

Joe got up from his easy chair and went over to where she stood. It was only three steps but Jeff recognized the symbolism in each one. He took the letters from his wife's fingers. 'Thank you, darling,' he said sheepishly, kissing her on the nose.

Sadie smiled, and returned to her kitchen domain.

Joe looked at his eldest son and grinned. 'She loves me really,' he said with an impudent glint in his eyes. He took the letters to the table, smoothed the creases out of the thick paper, and began to read, a surprised expression on his craggy face. Jeff was anxious to take a look.

'Time flies,' Joe remarked, shaking his head. Satisfied he had the date order correct he offered one to Jeff. 'This is the last one he sent.'

Jeff examined the letter, showed it to Clem. The writing was strong and neat, the date was 10th October 1859. 'Pa, this letter's nearly six years old.'

Joe shrugged and smiled. 'Guess neither of us is much for writing.'

'Did you write back?' Jeff asked.

'Maybe. Can't say for sure,' Joe told his son, adding, 'probably did.'

Clem and Jeff exchanged amused glances with Dan.

'Want me to write the letter, Pa?' Jeff suggested. 'You can sign it.'

'Good idea,' Joe answered.

'That's settled. I'll write it after supper.'

Pa Jackson was right about his wife not being exactly overjoyed when she heard about her sons' decision.

'Jefferson Jackson,' she chided, tears welling up in her eyes. 'You have only just got home, now you're fixing to leave again, and taking Clement with you.'

Jeff guessed she rounded on him because he was the oldest; she just hugged Clem, and stroked his straw-coloured hair.

* * *

Dan was waiting at the appointed place on the St Louis road on the edge of town; he was accompanied by another rider. 'This young feller's Billy Welch, a kinda second cousin.' Dan removed his brand-new black

21

Stetson and wiped the sweat from his brow. 'Hope you won't mind him tagging along?'

Clem and Jeff examined the youngster closely; he couldn't have been more than fifteen. Billy was tall for his age. The horse he sat on was too small for him, his feet weren't clearing the ground by much and the kid was stick thin.

'How old are you, boy?' Clem asked.

'Seventeen,' the youth bristled, 'and don't call me boy. The name's Billy.'

'OK. Hold your temper. No offence meant.'

Dan interjected, 'Is it OK for him to come along? I'm staking him. He's strong, for a kid,' he added. Billy bristled again at Dan's choice of words. 'He can ride and shoot, and the way I figured, four is better than three.'

It didn't take much figuring. 'OK by me,' Jeff said.

'Me too,' smiled Clem.

Billy's face broke into an enormous grin; he spurred his horse over and offered his hand.

'You won't regret it,' he said. His handshake was firm and purposeful; Jeff guessed that Billy was stronger than he looked.

3

Fort Benton, Montana

Fort Benton was a typical frontier town, a ramshackle mix of unpainted timber buildings, its broad main street ankle-deep in mud following a series of heavy storms.

After settling the horses in the livery stable, the boys sought out the best hotel the settlement could offer. Jeff's throat was dry as parchment and he announced he was going for a beer. The others turned down his invitation to join him, saying they just wanted to get some sleep.

In the smart saloon bar of the hotel, Jeff ordered. He stood at the bar and raised the glass to his lips, pleased the drink was refreshingly cool. A minute or so later the saloon doors swung open and closed behind an old trapper — a man with so much luxuriant facial hair that only his eyes, nose, plus a little of his high cheekbones were visible. He was dressed traditionally in fringed buckskin and a coonskin cap and carried a long Kentucky rifle. Canvas bags on crossbelts hung from both shoulders.

The trapper leaned the rifle against the bar. 'Whiskey,' he said, fumbling in his pockets. A leather poke dropped onto the beer-stained floor as the trapper searched for a coin. Jeff picked up the poke, politely handing it to the old man.

'Thankee kindly, pardner,' the trapper said. 'Buy you a drink?'

'That's OK,' Jeff replied, 'you don't have to.'

'Heck. I know that,' responded the trapper, 'but I want to. Don't meet many polite fellers these days.'

Jeff gave in and accepted. 'Make it a small one.'

The old man raised his shot-glass in the air. 'Here's to health, wealth, and all you could wish for a good friend.'

Jeff responded. 'Amen to that,' he said, shuddering as the fiery spirit threatened to burn the lining off the back of his throat.

'I like you, young feller. Have another?' The trapper poured out two more whiskeys before Jeff could refuse.

Jeff took a sip just to be friendly then nudged the shot-glass to the side. He leaned a forearm on the bar, and examined his new friend closely.

The man's wizened face was lined, his tanned skin like sunburned leather. His hands showed all the signs of hard graft, fingers gnarled, most looked like they had been broken at one time or another. His grubby buckskin tunic and trousers showed signs of wear. At odds with the other visible evidence the man's moccasins looked almost brand new. With each movement the trapper gave off an odour so pungent as to wrinkle Jeff's nose.

'You live around here?' the mountain man enquired.

'No. Just passing through,' replied Jeff.

'Where ya headed?'

'South,' Jeff answered, 'along the Missouri, towards the headwaters.'

'Huh? South, you say?'

'Yes.'

'Hmm.' The trapper scratched his nose. 'South?'

'Yes.' Jeff didn't much care for the way the trapper was quizzing him.

'You alone?'

'No. Me and my brother, plus two cousins.'

'Might be an idea to postpone your trip.'

'Ain't gonna happen,' said Jeff.

'Son. I ain't the kind of feller who usually gives out free advice, but I got some for ya.'

'Advice?' Jeff was puzzled.

'I jest come along the Missouri valley. Seen lots of sign. Injuns makin' a heap big trouble down thataway.' The trapper considered his next pronouncement carefully. 'If'n ya want to keep yer hair,

I'd steer well clear of the river road.'

For a moment Jeff pondered the trapper's warning. 'Indians, eh?'

'Yep. Blackfoot, Shoshone, Arapaho, plus some Cheyenne.'

Jeff took a slug of the whiskey; he felt like cursing loudly. 'Guess we'll have to hole up here till we get the all-clear.'

The trapper's eyes lit up. 'Not if you kin follow a map,' he chortled.

'I can. Why?'

'There's a way around. I got a map. You kin make a copy. I'll get it. Wait here.'

Jeff considered what the old man had said. He wasn't sure, but decided there was no harm in listening. The trapper disappeared through the saloon doors, and was back in no time at all, clutching an oilskin bag.

'Let's go sit at that table in the corner,' suggested the trapper, picking up his rifle, the whiskey bottle and shot-glasses with surprising dexterity.

Once at the table he removed a large, folded piece of parchment from the bag, and smoothed it out. Jeff could see that the map was well used; the corners were all dog-eared.

'Here's Fort Benton,' said the trapper, tracing an imaginary line over the map with a stab of his index finger. Jeff noticed the tip to the first knuckle of the trapper's right forefinger was missing. 'An' here's roughly where the Injuns'll most likely be.'

Jeff nodded.

The trapper continued, 'You wanna keep clear of that by at least thirty miles. Injuns got a lot of huntin' to get done before winter. I seen lots of sign of buffalo, so that's what they'll be focusin' their attention on. With me so far?' He grinned.

Jeff grunted.

'So, here's your alternative route.' Jeff leaned forward to get a better look.

'From here, head due south. You'll hit a range of hills called the Little Belt Mountains. There's a good pass through 'em at this time of year, good landmarks you can't miss. Three pointed peaks about fifty feet high, here.' He stabbed the map again. 'Hang on a minute, I'll get some paper and a pencil.'

Again the trapper shot off and was back in a few minutes.

'Got some from the hotel clerk.' He grinned, setting about to draw the promised copy.

Jeff watched as the trapper's steady hand drew lines on the paper; he had to admit, the old fellow had a talent for map-making.

'Army's building a new fort here,' he pointed, 'don't have a name yet as fer as I know.'

'That's where we're headed. I believe it'll be called Fort Ellis.'

'Right,' said the trapper. 'Good spot for a fort. There's a new wagon trail near there, opened up by ol' Johnny Bozeman. Pour us another while I git this done.'

Jeff poured one for the trapper, but declined to take more himself.

The trapper looked up and smiled

broadly. 'She's finished,' he said proudly, admiring his handiwork.

The map — a veritable work of art, spread over three pages, each with a link to the next — was better than the original because of the detail the old man had put into it. The trapper went through the route and its landmarks in great detail; Jeff made additional notes on the map then slid the original back inside its oilskin cover.

'Well, son . . . ' The trapper yawned, stretching out his long arms and his neck, amidst many sounds of joints clicking. 'I gotta get me some sleep. So I'll be sayin' goodnight.' He stood up, stretched again, then retrieved his belongings.

Jeff grabbed the man's hand, and pumped it. 'Thanks, Mr . . . ' He suddenly realized he'd never even asked the trapper his name.

The trapper anticipated what Jeff was about to say. 'Jim Bridger.'

Jeff recognized the name; he had heard stories of this man's exploits.

Trapper, frontiersman, lawman, army scout, the list seemed endless.

'Jeff Jackson. May I call you Jim?'

'Sure you kin. Be honoured.'

'Thanks, er, Jim,' Jeff said. 'Are the stories about you true?'

Jim Bridger smiled. 'Some, maybe. Some maybe not.'

Jeff had still got hold of Bridger's hand. 'Jim, I'm much obliged to you for what you've done.'

'Heck, Jeff, it weren't nothin' really. I wish you and your kin all the luck in the world. See you again maybe.'

Jim Bridger waved once as he exited the saloon. 'So long,' he called out.

'Jim Bridger,' Jeff whispered, as he headed to his room — tingling inside, thrilled to have met a western legend.

4

The hair on the back of Jeff's neck had prickled for more than an hour. He recognized the familiar uneasy feeling he'd felt many times during the war. He reined in Atlas. The big black's ears were up, ignoring the luxuriant purple sage covering the bed of the deep draw. Jeff turned in the saddle, placing a finger to his lips, motioning to his companions to come closer.

'Keep your eyes peeled. I got a funny feeling,' he said softly. 'Dan, you and Billy drop back aways.'

Clem and Dan respected Jeff's uncanny sixth sense; Billy looked puzzled, but nodded.

The draw widened to nigh on a hundred feet, the ground strewn with smooth boulders interspersed with grass and sage. In the distance a small coppice of slender-trunked birch trees added a splash of green to the sandy landscape. Ahead, where the draw narrowed sharply, Jeff watched a thin cloud of dust rise from behind the ridge. Might be nothing. Might be dust whipped up by a gust of wind. Might be Indians.

Jeff twisted in the saddle, pointing to a second cloud of dust, this one more intense. The draw twisted sharply left around a protuberance of rocks and trees.

'Where you boys headed?' a deep, gravelly voice boomed out; the shouter of the challenge was not visible.

Jeff and Clem pulled up short. Now they saw who had spoken. He was a big man, framed in shadow, sitting astride a fine-looking palomino. The picture became clearer as the dust settled. Hidden from the trail by a patch of dense foliage were four other riders.

Dan slowed his horse to a walk, unable to make out the shouted challenge. Finger to his lips he gestured to Billy to halt. Dan slipped his Spencer repeater from the saddle holster and dismounted quietly; Billy yanked out his big Sharps rifle and did the same.

Dan handed over the reins of his mount. 'Stay here,' he ordered in a hushed tone.

Billy was none too pleased to be excluded, but nodded his agreement to stay put.

Dan inched forward, careful the jingle of his spurs didn't give away his presence. Stetson removed, Dan peered over a large boulder; he couldn't see much for dust.

Jeff hovered his hand near his six-gun. 'Mister,' he called out, 'I don't take kindly to being sneaked up on, especially by people I can't see. C'mon out from under them trees.'

The big man edged the palomino into the open. Jeff recognized the grey of the Confederacy and three dirty gold letters on the man's battered cavalry hat — CSA.

'Now you see me.' The man's eyes and forehead were dark in the shadow of his hat. 'And my friends,' he added sombrely through blackened teeth, framed by an unkempt, long and bushy black moustache and beard, his accent a slow southern drawl; it looked like the man's face and hands hadn't seen water for some time.

The four other riders walked their horses alongside the big man, all dressed in dirty, well-worn Confederate uniforms.

'I'd be obliged if you would answer my question,' the big man challenged.

Without answering Jeff and Clem dismounted slowly.

The big man tried to keep his voice even and stress free.

'I asked where you're headed,' he repeated.

'Fort Ellis,' Jeff answered curtly.

'Ain't no such place,' the big man snarled, a long white scar now clearly visible from his ear to the corner of his jaw.

'It's under construction,' Jeff told him confidently, 'we got business there.'

'Where is it?'

'On the Yellowstone. North of Gallatin City.'

'That a fact?'

Jeff nodded.

'What business you got there?'

Jeff had had enough; his hackles were
steadily coming to the boil. He watched
the big man's eyes wander over the
string of horses that were now calmly
chomping at the grass and sage.

'Nice meeting you fellers,' Jeff said
politely, 'but we need to get moving.'

The big man held up a hand. 'Not so
fast, feller.'

Jeff slipped the leather thong off the
hammer of his six-gun.

'This is our territory. Free passage is
prohibited, unless you've paid the toll.'

'Which is?' Jeff enquired.

'One dollar a head. Cows, horses, or
men, makes no difference.'

'Seems a mite steep, wouldn't you
say, Clem?'

'Extortionate,' Clem answered. 'I
don't think we should pay.'

Dan heard every word of the exchange.

Billy arrived at Dan's side having tied the horses securely. Dan stood, the momentary silence broken by the well-oiled lever of the Spencer repeating rifle grating with mechanical precision as a cartridge clicked into place, followed by the metallic sound of the Spencer being cocked. 'Take your weapons out slowly and toss them over here,' Dan ordered.

For a moment no one moved, then the big man's right hand swept down towards his holster; it never reached its intended destination.

The Spencer barked out a sharp crack, the bullet taking the big man in the right shoulder. The palomino reared, pitching its rider from the saddle. Two other horses reared; others skittered around, panic in their eyes.

Billy showed himself and fired into the air to still any aggressive movement in the four other men. Hat gone, the big man's face was clear now, dust smeared his beard, he clutched his shoulder with his left hand, crimson blood oozed between his calloused fingers. His nervous comrades stared down the barrel of Jeff's and Clem's pistols that had appeared in their hands in a blur of movement. One by one the four Copperheads raised their hands above their heads. One mean-looking individual with a sharp-featured weasel face threatened to go for his gun until a second bullet from Dan's Spencer rang out, the bullet tearing a chunk of leather out of the man's saddle horn.

'Anyone else want to taste lead?' Dan yelled, striding forward, Billy close behind.

The big man grimaced, the veins in his neck stood out as the blood pounded through them; he was obviously in a great deal of pain. He looked up at Jeff, eyeing him contemptuously. 'One day, mister, you'll be sorry your friend didn't kill me,' he threatened, defiantly.

Dan poked the Spencer into the

man's chest. 'Best shut up, pilgrim, or I might just take it into my head to finish you now.'

The big man snarled out a string of curses and threats.

'You Johnny Rebs are about as scary as a newborn kitten,' Dan said.

'Step down from your horses. And keep your hands where we can see 'em,' Jeff ordered.

The four men dismounted, anxious to know their fate.

'Help your boss.' Jeff pointed to the big man.

Two men stepped forward. They lifted the obvious leader of their pack of rebel jaspers and carried him to the shade of a tree, leaning his back against the trunk.

Dan prodded another of the men. 'You,' he said. 'Collect the weapons from your buddies and put them here.' He motioned to a spot on the ground. 'Any sudden move and I'll blast you to hell. Understand?'

The man nodded sullenly and got on

with his task. Billy brought up the horses.

Dan kept the Spencer trained on the captives. The man tending to the leader of the rebels pulled open the big man's cavalry blouse and mopped the steady flow of blood with a thin towel Dan had allowed him to fetch from his saddlebag. He turned his head to look at Dan. 'Wound looks clean; bullet went right through,' he pronounced, spitting on a small piece of moss and jamming it into the bullet hole. He bandaged the wound tightly with a strip of material he'd cut from part of the towel. The big man fainted as the bandage tightened. The would-be nurse stood up, admiring his handiwork. 'Be good as new in a few weeks,' he said to no one in particular.

'Splash some water on his face,' ordered Jeff.

The big man came round with a groan. He opened his eyes slowly. 'Water,' he pleaded.

'Give him some,' ordered Jeff.

'OK to give him something stronger?'

the rebel soldier asked.

Jeff nodded his approval. A bottle of spirits was produced and held to the big man's lips; he took a long pull at the bottle, never for one second taking his hate-filled eyes off Jeff. The soldier slapped the cork back into the bottle, and wiped the big man's mouth with his sleeve. He turned to Jeff. 'Want a pull?'

'No, thanks.'

The rebel soldier looked in Jeff's direction. 'What have you got in mind for us, Mister?' His eyes were pleading. 'You gonna hang us?'

The question surprised Jeff. 'Reb,' he said, 'that's about what you jayhawkers deserve.'

The man and his companions stiffened noticeably, suddenly fearful of the possibility of having their necks stretched. For a moment Jeff feared that they might panic and do something stupid.

'There'll be no hanging,' he said quickly, immediately sensing the relief from the rebels, and from his own companions. 'But,' he added, 'I want each of you to swear to quit Montana and head west. Whatdya say?'

The relieved confederates exchanged hurried glances.

'We agree,' answered the man who had tended the big man's wound.

The big man scowled.

'Good,' pronounced Jeff. 'You can keep your horses and belongings. I'll even let you keep your guns, but we'll take most of your ammunition. I'll leave you a few rounds in case you run into any Indians.'

All but one of the rebels chorused their thanks.

'Remember. I don't expect to see you again, but if I do, I'll kill you.' No one could misunderstand the harsh tone in Jeff's voice. 'Make sure that's all clear in your minds.'

Neither Clem nor Dan had ever heard Jeff speak so.

Jeff looked across at the big man. Allowing for the fact that he was in pain, Jeff felt the man's hatred; this was one son-of-a-bitch that he would not trust an inch.

Clem sidled over to his brother. 'Jeff. You sure that's the right thing to do with these boys?'

Jeff looked into his brother's eyes. 'What's the alternative?' he challenged. 'You want to kill them?'

'No! No way,' Clem answered indignantly. 'I just thought maybe we'd take 'em with us. Hand 'em over to the army. That's all.'

'You want that responsibility?' There was anger in Jeff's challenge. 'If they try to escape, you gonna shoot them?'

'No,' replied Clem. 'Aw, I just . . . Oh, I don't know.' Clem was embarrassed. 'I just thought — '

Jeff cut his brother off in midsentence. 'Let me do the thinking, little brother.'

This was a side of Jeff Clem hadn't seen before and he didn't like it. At that moment he could have easily struck his brother.

Clem skulked away as Jeff added, 'In any case, what would the army do with them?'

Clem shot an angry glance over his shoulder. 'OK, you made your point.'

Jeff bunched his fists in anger — with himself, not with his brother. He knew how harsh his words must have sounded. He felt again that old familiar feeling — the pressure of command was once again bearing down hard on his shoulders. He would have to make it up with Clem. He knew it, but now wasn't the time; these rebels needed to be convinced he meant what he said.

Jeff watched until the silhouettes of the five Johnny Rebs disappeared over the horizon; he hoped to have seen the last of the big man with the long white scar. He mounted Atlas and kicked the big horse forward. 'Let's move out,' he called out.

The beaming smile broadened across Billy's face; he'd been involved in his first gunfight, he couldn't wait for the excitement to repeat itself.

5

Off to the south from behind a round-topped hill a pall of black smoke plumed skywards, blackening the horizon.

The four riders reined in their mounts, watching the hues of grey and black swirl in the light breeze.

'That's more than a brush fire,' ventured Dan.

'Let's go take a look. Somebody might need help,' Clem said, his depressed mood improving.

Jeff was cautious. 'Hold on,' he barked, 'we don't know what's over that hill.' He examined the three disappointed expressions. 'Yes, we'll take a look, but we need to approach with caution. No need to go galloping in like a bunch of virgin cavalrymen.' The others knew he was right. 'Clem. You and Dan work your way over to the east. Me and Billy'll approach from the north. Keep inside the tree line where you can. Be careful. And quiet,' he added.

The hillside proved to be much steeper than Jeff had imagined; the horses needed a firm hand, but Atlas proved as sure-footed as ever. After weaving in and out of firs and stubby scrub-oaks, Jeff and Billy reached a flattened-out ridge. Their mounts snorted, happy to get a breather. Jeff stood tall in his stirrups and peered over the deep-green foliage of a large bush.

The knot tightened in his stomach as he took in the scene. The smoke was coming from a group of burned-out buildings. The remnants of charred timbers and blackened, earth-sod walls had once been someone's home. Jeff scanned the area slowly, his eyes periodically resting on a bush or another piece of cover, not moving on until he was sure no hostile elements were around; he knew Clem would be doing the same. Satisfied, he tugged the Spencer from the saddle holster near his left knee then turned Atlas's head.

'C'mon, Billy. Keep your eyes peeled.'

The two riders walked their horses out of a stand of scrub-oaks, all the time looking around cautiously. A couple of hundred yards to his left Clem and Dan emerged from a copse of firs, rifles in hand. Dan raised a hand. Jeff signalled to meet at the largest smoking building.

About fifty feet from what Jeff took to have once been a barn, the prone body of a man lay spreadeagled on the ground, arrows stuck out at various angles from the body; the man had been scalped. Jeff dismounted, going down on one knee to take a closer look. Billy threw up.

There was a well nearby.

'Go take a drink of water,' Jeff advised, 'but check the well ain't been fouled.'

Clem and Dan walked their mounts

to where Jeff was kneeling. The cousins dismounted.

'Indians?' asked Dan, stating the obvious.

'Looks like it,' Jeff commented.

Something he couldn't explain was nagging at the back of his mind.

They tied their horses to a branch.

'Billy,' Dan called out, 'you OK?'

Billy turned, his face a mixture of white and green. 'Never seen anythin' like that before,' he said, fighting back the nausea.

'You stay with the horses,' Jeff said to the young man, 'we'll take a look around.'

Billy didn't need asking twice.

'Door's been smashed in.' Clem pointed to the opening in the wall of the building where a rough-sawn door was hanging off one leather hinge.

Jeff moved towards the smouldering ruins. He stepped inside. A tangle of charred timber beams lay at odd angles where they had fallen when the roof had collapsed. Even without a roof the interior was still pretty dark. The smell of burnt flesh was horrendous.

The horrific sight that greeted Jeff was hard to look at even for the most battle-scarred eyes: the charred body of a once pretty young woman, clothes torn away, her bruised and bloodied features distorted. A few strands of blood-soaked light-brown hair spilled across one naked shoulder; a bright scarlet slash across the top of her forehead where the rest of her scalp had once sat.

The bile deep in Jeff's stomach threatened to erupt as Billy's had; he managed by sheer willpower to control it, but not before he sampled the awful and well-remembered taste.

'Stay out of here.' He shouted the order as Clem's shadow appeared. 'Stay out!'

Jeff turned, a tear in his eye, wished not to be seeing the all too vivid pictures in his imagination. He knew full well what had happened. The evidence of man's lustful fury was plain to see. Jeff covered the body with his coat.

He pushed past Clem in the doorway. 'Gimme some water,' he shouted to Dan.

Clem peered into the gloom, seeing what had so revolted his brother.

Jeff drank until the canteen was drained.

'Nobody round back,' Billy offered. His face had returned to its normally healthy colour. 'But,' he continued, 'there's lots of arrows around, an' there's a dead dog and horse in the corral, an' a dead steer, all shot.' Billy paused. 'I think there's another dog somewhere, wounded maybe. I was sure I heard it whimpering or something.'

'No Indians did this,' Jeff stated. 'Indians wouldn't kill a horse, or a cow, they'd take 'em.' Clem and Dan leaned in closer. 'Another thing. Check the flights and bindings on those arrows.' He pointed. 'They're all different. I'm no expert on Indians, but I do know that every tribe has their own signature on stuff like that.'

Jeff stood up, slapped the dust from his jeans with his hat. What Billy had said just began to register. 'An animal whimpering, you said?'

Billy nodded. 'Yes.'

'Where? Show me.'

Billy led the way around the remains of the house; three animal corpses lay where Billy had described. 'Here, I guess,' the young man said.

'Take a look around,' Jeff said, hearing nothing but the breeze and the pounding of his own heartbeat. Other sounds now drifted on the wind: sounds of timbers being moved around, hoisted and dropped, the occasional scrape of metal upon metal as the four men searched.

Near a back wall of the house, Dan's boot heel banged loudly on timber. He looked down, saw only earth — bare except for a few hardy stalks of grass. He stamped, but instead of the dull sound of boot on soil he heard the unmistakable sound of boot on wood. He brushed away the soil with his leather-gloved hand. Under half an inch of soil was a timber board. Dan looked down at his discovery, figuring he was probably standing on a root cellar. He was about to clear away all of the covering of earth when the silence was broken by the sound Billy had described.

'Found it!' Dan called out, still not knowing exactly what it was. The three others crowded round, peering over Dan's shoulder; all was suddenly eerily quiet.

Dan located an edge of the boarding and tugged, but it wouldn't budge; it was stubbornly stuck fast. He looked up at Billy and said, 'Find me something to use to prise this thing up.'

Billy handed over part of an old shovel. The creak of a nail coming loose preceded the lifting of the board; that was when Dan saw the camouflaged hasp and staple at the opposite end to where he was lifting. He removed the staple, flipped over the hasp and raised the boarding, which revealed itself to be a door-like fabrication, around four feet by two feet. The chasm into which four sets of eyes strained was dark and foreboding. Spiders climbed the sods of earth lining the hole, irked at having their web-spinning tranquillity disturbed by the four giants that had intruded into their existence.

A crude ladder of rough timber logs disappeared into the inkiness. 'Give me some room,' demanded Dan as he set one booted foot onto the top of the ladder, transferring more weight to test the safety of the structure. 'Seems strong enough.'

One step followed another until only the crown of Dan's hat was visible. He ducked under the overhang, disappearing from view. A loud expletive followed the sound of his toe striking a rock or something. 'Sure is dark down here.'

'Careful there ain't any raccoons in there,' said Clem.

'Or ghosts,' laughed Billy.

'Shut your mouth, Billy.' Dan struck a match. 'Tunnel goes back t'ward the house.' The intense light from the match died away.

'Billy, go down and help Dan,' Jeff ordered.

Billy shied away. 'No, sir, I ain't venturin' down there, gives me the creeps.'

'I'll go,' volunteered Clem. He wrapped a hunk of dry grass around a stick then lit it. He followed in Dan's footsteps, his head reappearing for a second. 'There's a room down here, and another ladder.'

'In the house,' came the shout.

Jeff ran back to the doorway, gesturing to Billy to stay out. He was in time to see a charred rush mat being pushed up. The mat slipped away, revealing the trapdoor Dan was pushing from underneath, his beaming, soot-smudged face a picture of happiness.

'Jeff!' Dan's excited voice echoed through the debris. 'We've found . . . a baby!' He swallowed hard, as though not believing his own words. 'A baby,' Dan shouted, 'we've found a little baby!'

★ ★ ★

'Yes, sir. It's a right neighbourly thing you fellers done. Folks, a toast. Raise your glasses to these four Christian boys.'

The rotund gentleman speaking the words was the newly elected mayor of the small civilian settlement on the north bank of the Yellowstone River near Fort Ellis.

People cheered, some of them already drunk as a skunk. Almost the entire population had gathered in the three-quarters-built saloon to hail the four heroes who had saved the life of baby Abigail Trenton.

The swaddled babe had been found in a tiny cot, lying on a pile of documents and letters proclaiming her identity and her next of kin, and a small canvas bag containing ten gold pieces.

The couple had kin in the town who said they would raise the child as their own.

Jeff presented his compliments, along with the evidence, to the senior officer at Fort Ellis, Major Ryan. His chief scout, a Crow Indian, confirmed Jeff's belief that no Indian would use arrows with four different markings. Nor would they waste bullets on them. Major Ryan confirmed that the attack would be investigated, and the US Marshal in Virginia City would be informed.

After dinner in his quarters, Major Ryan read through the army contract Jeff showed him and nodded. 'I'm expecting infantry, plus a troop of cavalry to arrive within the next month. The new garrison commander will be delighted that someone in Washington has had the good sense to realize the need for remounts.'

'Will you be remaining here?' Clem enquired.

'No. As soon as our work here is

finished my men and I will be moving on to Fort C. F. Smith to strengthen the fortifications there.'

'Perhaps we'll meet again, Major; our contract also includes an order to provide remounts to Fort Smith.'

'Let us hope so,' the major said cordially. 'Now if you will excuse me, I need to get some sleep. I'll come to the gate tomorrow to wish you Godspeed.' He pushed back his chair and said goodnight.

6

Double-J ranch

The well-marked trail wound between juniper bush and gorse-clad hills, following the course of fast-flowing streams and rivers. Healthy stands of lodgepole pine, blue spruce and Douglas fir lined the slopes, standing proudly amongst an array of colourful wild flowers.

It hadn't rained one spot since the riverboat had landed them in Fort Benton and today there was little breeze to cool the heavy warm air, making for uncomfortable travel.

The four riders took a break by a fast-flowing brook. Jeff took out Jim Bridger's map and smoothed the paper out on a flat rock. 'Reckon we're about here,' he prodded the map, 'so should be there in a coupla hours.'

After around thirty minutes, they

remounted and continued their journey. Soon the pretty valley widened considerably, and a number of grazing cattle came into view.

The rough trail rose steadily above the level of the river, the landscape now one of rolling hills covered in endless forests of fir trees framed by distant, blue-hazed, snowcapped mountains.

As they breasted a steep rise, Billy pointed to the green valley stretching out below them. 'Look, buildings. Must be the place? Right?'

'Guess so,' replied Jeff, feeling a surge of excitement.

The distant buildings became clearer as the four tired riders drew nearer: a large ranch house, barn, various out-buildings, plus split-rail fencing and corrals.

The sign read Double-J Ranch. The prominent letters were burned deep into the wood.

Off to their left, in a small, fenced-off field, a few Longhorns plus a couple of white-faced Herefords stared cautiously at the riders.

The impressive Double-J ranch house was a sprawling affair, with a wide porch and a portico of arches running the length of the building. A long, single-storey bunkhouse sat to one side, with a tall, red-painted barn set away from the house on the opposite side of the expansive yard. Around the perimeter were a number of small sheds.

Billy leaned over the neck of his horse to lift the looped leather strap holding the gate shut. As the gate swung open a large yellow dog with a red and white spotted necktie round its neck came hurtling down the track, barking excitedly to send the unrecognized visitors packing. Billy whistled at the dog, calling softly. The animal suddenly stood calmly. Billy leaned down and called the dog to him, clicking the fingers of his gloved hand whilst cooing an odd mixture of sounds. The dog walked over, its tail wagging furiously, and allowed Billy to stroke its head and ears.

'Dogs love him,' Dan informed his two cousins. 'Never seen one that didn't.'

'That's obvious,' said Clem.

Billy closed the gate and the four friends walked their horses towards the ranch house.

A tall, bareheaded, heavy-set man toting a double-barrelled shotgun appeared in the doorway of the ranch house. He stepped purposely out onto the porch. A slim cowboy wearing a wide sombrero emerged from the barn.

The man stepped slowly down the porch steps. 'Identify yourselves. Friends are welcome.' The menace in the voice was at odds with the sentiment being expressed.

Jeff took it upon himself to answer. 'Name's Jeff Jackson.'

The man walked forward two or three steps. 'Jeff Jackson?' he asked incredulously.

'Yes, sir.' Jeff waved his hand towards his three cohorts. 'And, if you are Jim

Jackson, we are your kin.'

'Kin?'

Jeff nodded. 'Mind if we step down?'

The perplexed expression remained on the man's broad face. He lowered the shotgun. 'Sure,' he said.

Jeff dismounted and took off his hat, brushed back his sweat-soaked hair, and took off one leather glove. After wiping his hand on the leg of his jeans Jeff held it out towards the man.

'I'm the son of your cousin, Joe Jackson,' Jeff explained. 'Pa wrote you a letter.'

'Letter?' the man repeated. 'Ain't had no letter.'

'Oh.' Jeff's disappointment showed. 'Are you Jim Jackson?' he asked politely.

The man nodded. He looked deep into Jeff's brown eyes, the first signs of understanding beginning to show on his unshaven face. 'Joe Jackson's boy?'

Jim Jackson dropped the shotgun onto the ground, grabbing Jeff in a bear hug that threatened to squeeze the life out of him.

'Joe Jackson's boy,' he repeated, 'well, I'll be . . . '

Jeff smiled broadly, wheezing out, 'One of 'em.' He turned his head. 'That big feller there is my brother, Clem, and the good-looking one is our cousin, Dan Jackson,' he said, trying his best to recover his breath.

'Archie's boy?'

Dan nodded. He and Clem dismounted.

Jim gave Clem and Dan a repeat of the bear-hug treatment.

'This young feller — c'mon, Billy, step down,' Jeff coaxed, 'is Billy Welch. He's a cousin of Dan's on his ma's side.' Billy got the bear-hug treatment too.

For some time Jim Jackson was speechless. He examined the four well-set-up young men facing him, and slapped his forehead. 'Well, if this don't beat all.' Jim scratched his head. 'My-oh-my, three more Jacksons. Plus one,' Jim added, looking at Billy. 'Let's go into the house.' He turned to lead the way, shouting for the cowboy standing near the barn to tend to the visitors' horses.

The four visitors removed their spurs, stamped their dusty boots and dusted off their clothes as best they could before stepping across the threshold. The temperature inside the well-furnished ranch house was much cooler than outside. Jim Jackson motioned for his unexpected visitors to sit; all four accepted a glass of cool lemonade.

'So, tell me, what are you boys doing this far west?' asked Jim.

Jeff told Jim he was sorry his father's letter hadn't arrived then went on to explain how and why they had come to Montana; Jim was overjoyed to learn of the boys' plans.

'Well, that's settled. An' I'm not taking no for an answer,' Jim Jackson insisted. 'You're all stayin' here for as long as you like.' Jim smiled an avuncular smile. 'We got plenty of room. Anyway,' he shrugged, 'you're kin, so you can't refuse.' Jim turned his head as the tall grandfather clock in the corner struck four o'clock. 'Ika and the kids'll be back soon,' Jim stated. The boys exchanged surprised glances. 'She's half Crow Indian,' Jim added. 'Ika's my wife,' Jim announced proudly. 'We got two kids, you'll love them too.'

Jeff broke the momentary awkward silence. 'Is Ika your wife's Indian name?'

'Yes,' Jim answered enthusiastically, hoping to take the embarrassment out of the situation. 'Her full Indian name is Ika Phangyang.' Jim took in the puzzled expressions. 'The rough translation means . . . ' He paused, trying to find the best way to describe the meaning. 'It's not easy to translate literally; there's nothing like it in English.'

Jeff could see Jim was having trouble.

'You know when grass is beaten down by a strong breeze?'

'Like a grassy field on a windy day?' Jeff suggested.

'Exactly!' exclaimed Jim, a broad smile spreading across his weather-beaten face. 'I like to think of it as like a strong warm breeze. Guess I'm a big old romantic at heart.'

'Do you speak the Crow language?'

'Some. I lived with the Crow on and off for a few years.'

'What are your kids' names?' Clem asked.

'My daughter's Crow name is Bili-taachiia. It translates to Moon. I call her Mo. She likes to be called Sarah; that's her baptismal name.' He laughed. 'In English my boy's Indian name is Grey Wolf. In Crow it's Cheete Choose. He was baptized Jason.'

Jim spelled out the names for the boys; each made a clumsy attempt at the pronunciation amidst peals of laughter.

Jim showed the boys around the house and the bedrooms they would share — Jeff with Clem, Dan with Billy.

The place was enormous, clean and tidy, well furnished, not at all the picture of a frontier dwelling Jeff had in his mind.

In the large kitchen, a series of appetizing smells emanated from three or four large, steaming pots on a huge cooking range, and another surprise greeted the boys. Jim made the introductions.

'This smiling oriental gentleman is Cheng Li.' The Chinaman bowed deeply. 'Cheng Li's from someplace called Shanghai,' Jim added.

All except Billy had heard of the place. Only Jeff knew where it was.

Cheng Li looked innocent as Jim turned to face him. 'What's for dinner?'

'Steak an' taters,' Cheng Li answered, 'same as usua'.' He grinned, turning back to tend his pots.

Jim laughed loudly. 'Take no notice of him. We don't always eat steak. Sometimes we have beef stew, or roast beef.' He leaned towards the boys, his voice not much louder than a whisper.

'I'm not sure Cheng Li knows how to cook much else.'

Billy piped up. 'Chicken?' he suggested. 'There's lots of 'em in the yard.'

'Sometimes. But only if I ask,' Jim sighed.

Cheng Li spun round. 'You no say you want chicken,' he protested. 'You want chicken?' Jim's face was a picture of puzzlement. 'You want chicken, you say you want chicken.' The Chinaman chided, 'Cheng Li no a mind-leader.'

'OK,' said Jim, 'chicken tomorrow.'

'How you want? Flied, boyed. China style?' Cheng Li seemed determined to make Jim feel awkward.

Jim waved a hand in a sweeping motion. 'Oh, I dunno. Fried. OK?'

The Chinaman stood, legs apart, arms folded across his chest. 'See? You say, Cheng Li do.'

'Aw.' Jim's exasperation showed clear. 'Come on, let's take a look outside.'

The interior of the tall barn was dark and dusty; bits of straw floated gently in the air. A bare-headed man who had been bending over a small animal stood and looked at the five men.

'Sanchez,' Jim called out. He motioned for the man to come over. 'This here's Jose-Maria Sanchez; his pa was Mexican.' The man flashed a smile of dazzling white teeth that contrasted with his swarthy features. 'Likes to be called Sanchez,' Jim added, then introduced the boys one by one.

'Welcome, señors,' Sanchez said, with only the faintest of an accent.

'He OK?' asked Jim, motioning to the animal the cowboy had been tending to.

'*Sí*. He's doing just fine.' Sanchez noticed Billy's curiosity, and added, 'Want to see?'

'Sure.' Billy tried not to sound overly enthusiastic.

The foal was newborn, only an hour or so old, russet-coloured, with a white blaze running the length of his head, and white stockings on his front legs.

'He's beautiful,' gasped Billy. 'Can I stroke him?'

Sanchez nodded like a proud father. 'Gently, though.'

Billy squatted next to the foal and put out a hand to stroke the animal's pink nose. The foal's big eyes lost their fear and evidently enjoyed the caress. It pushed its nose into Billy's hand demanding more of the same.

Billy suppressed a delighted giggle as he stroked and scratched the foal's ears and head. The foal's mother, a bay mare, whinnied and moved to its baby, as though to tell Billy that was enough. The ungainly foal struggled to its feet, tottered slightly before instinctively diving its nose towards one of his mother's teats.

The heavy drumming sound of horses approaching echoed around the ranch and barn.

'That'll be Ika,' Jim announced, leading the way out of the barn.

As the dust settled, the outline of three Indian ponies and their riders became clearer. A striking-looking Indian woman, dressed in patterned buckskin, sat astride a brown and white pinto. Her hair, black and glistening as a raven's wing, was tied in two long pigtails hanging either side of her tanned oval face; she looked to be in her late twenties, less than half Jim's age.

Swinging one long leg over the pony's neck she sprang from the animal's back. Raising one elegant hand she acknowledged her husband's wave. Jim rushed forward. Their kiss, and the embrace that followed, long and intimate, showed no sign of anything but the most natural behaviour. Jeff was sure that Jim was giving a demonstration for the benefit of his visitors; he was obviously proud of his young wife.

The dust had now all but settled, revealing the two other riders, both children; a pretty girl of about seven or eight, a younger version of her mother, and a long-haired boy a few years younger.

Jim broke off the embrace. Leaving one arm encircling Ika's slender waist, his face broke into a beaming smile.

'This is Ika,' he gushed, giving her a smacker of a kiss on the cheek, 'and these pair of imps are Sarah,' the girl smiled, 'and Jason.' The boy raised a hand.

Ika smiled warmly then shot an enquiring glance at her husband, who suddenly got her unspoken message.

'Sorry, darlin',' Jim chortled, 'these young fellers are my kin from back east. Sort of nephews, you might say.'

The couple walked to where the boys stood, hats removed.

Jeff took the lead. 'Jeff Jackson, ma'am,' he announced in a loud voice, beating Jim to the punch. Ika took Jeff's proffered hand and shook it politely. Then, still holding his hand, she placed her left hand on Jeff's shoulder for support and stood on tiptoe, kissing Jeff first on his right cheek then his left. Her lips were warm, soft and cushioned against his unshaven skin. Her hand, soft also, was slender and cool.

Ika's eyes sparkled mischievously.

'Welcome, Jeff. It's lovely to meet you,' she soothed.

Her refined accent and velvety voice brought the visitors up short; the surprise showed clear on each of their faces. Jeff felt his face colour as he gazed deep into Ika's beautiful velvet-brown eyes; he didn't want to break contact.

Ika let go of Jeff's hand, and moved a pace to the right to greet Clem.

'Clem Jackson, ma'am.'

Ika smiled knowingly, as one by one she greeted each of the visitors with equal intimate warmth. Dan announced his relationship to the brothers with a sloppy grin that spread from one ear to the other. Billy found it difficult to speak, his face blushing bright red.

Ika rounded on her husband. 'Jim! You never told me you had so many handsome nephews,' she purred, cementing the immediate and undying regard she had already won from the four visitors with her natural beauty and eloquent greeting.

'Let's go in the house,' Jim piped up, sensing the arrival of an embarrassing silence.

Ika turned to the children. 'Put away the ponies,' she told them with a smile, 'then wash your hands and face. Supper will be ready soon.' Ika glanced in the direction of the ranch house where Cheng Li had appeared, skillet in one hand.

'Twenty minute,' the Chinaman called out, his voice abrupt and lacking in patience. He opened the door and disappeared back into the ranch house.

Ika caught the bundle the boy threw to her. 'Now, gentlemen,' she looked at her husband's kinfolk expansively, 'I really must take my own advice. I need to wash and get out of these dirty clothes.' She swished through the ranch house door after flashing another sparkling smile.

Jeff, Clem, Dan and Billy were dumbstruck.

'Ain't she somethin'?' Jim called out, breaking the silence. He slapped Jeff, the nearest to him, on the shoulder. 'Well, what do you think?' Jim asked proudly.

Jeff crammed his hat on his head. 'She is beautiful.' As soon as the words had passed his lips Jeff was sure he had said the wrong thing.

Jim clapped Jeff on the shoulder. 'She sure is. Beautiful and intelligent,' he pronounced. 'One in a million. Let's go eat.'

Over dinner, Ika beguiled the four visitors with the story of how she and Jim had met, of her childhood, her education and beliefs. She spoke about her father, Red Hawk, hereditary war chief of the Crow, of her mother, and of her siblings.

★   ★   ★

Next morning Jim insisted on taking the boys on a tour of his ranch. He was obviously proud of what he had achieved since becoming a reluctant rancher. As the five men rode the boundary of the ranch Jim explained how many head of cattle he reckoned he owned. Not a precise science, he explained, because of the way cows wandered off, stubbornly refusing to stay where they were put. They paid a fleeting visit to two small farms neighbouring Jim's land.

'Mostly, we get along fine,' Jim announced, ' 'cept for one outfit — the Circle B. Owned by a big Scottish feller named Alexander Brown; his is the biggest spread in this part of the territory. He's a miserable so-and-so; never seen him so much as smile,' Jim added. 'Scowls mostly. Never satisfied, always wants more. Tried to get himself elected Mayor of White Bluff. Paid out a lot of cash . . . ' Jim chuckled. 'Didn't win, though. Made a packet during the war supplying beef to the Union Army; guess we all did well out of it. Army needed beef and plenty of it. Brown added considerably to the northern boundary of his spread at that time; got a number of government land grants.

Folks reckon he's in an all-fired hurry to get what he wants. Namely, to be the biggest rancher in the territory, and he don't seem too particular about how he does it.' Jim paused and shook his head. 'Seems to figure he owns the entire valley and that the rest of us ought to quit. He's already bought out a couple of the less successful farmers; paid less than their places was worth. Last one packed up a coupla weeks ago. Went back east.' He rubbed his chin. 'You'll know him when you see him: shock of red hair and beard. Big as a bear with mean eyes.'

'Sounds nasty,' commented Jeff.

Jim nodded. 'Ben, that's the farmer I mentioned, had his crops trampled, fences destroyed. Said it was no accident, blamed Alexander Brown's cowboys, but offered no proof. He said he wasn't prepared to stick around long enough to find out how far Brown would go, so he took what Brown offered.'

'Is it only the farmers that have suffered?'

'Heck no. Us ranchers haven't escaped. But it's mostly the farmers. Can't see why they bother, land around here ain't the best for farming. Seems certain that Brown applied more than a little pressure on the ones who quit. Another had his barn *accidentally* burned down.' He got thoughtful. 'Could've bin an accident, I guess. Either way it seemed a mite suspicious.' Jim's expression became more rueful. 'There's also been a couple of shootings.' He saw the questioning looks. 'Coupla cowboys lookin' for work got shot in town. Self-defence was the verdict. Also been one or two of Walter Schultz's cowboys beaten up. Walt owns the spread between mine and the Circle B. He's had the worst of it, including cattle-rustling. One thing after another.' Jim pulled a face. 'Brown don't seem the kind of bird to wait around to get what he wants, peaceable like.'

'Can't the law do anything?' asked Clem.

'Sheriff Todd went through the

motions, didn't find anythin', he said. Nobody expected him to anyway.'

'Why not?'

'Brown owns him.'

'You reckon this man Brown is behind these things?'

'Yep! But nobody can prove a thing,' Jim answered resignedly.

'Couldn't a US Marshal, or the army, do something?'

'Maybe. I heard a rumour that some of the farmers wrote to the governor. Schultz has been trying to get folks interested in starting a citizens' vigilante committee, but nothing's come of it so far.'

'You had any trouble?' asked Jeff.

'Some,' Jim said ruefully. 'Lost a few cows. Found a few last round-up looked like their brands had been altered. Good they were, but no doubt in my mind they'd been tampered with. Sheriff Todd all but called me a liar, then backed down, said he thought I was probably mistaken.' Jim spat out a stream of tobacco juice. 'I put it down to experience.' He saw questioning expressions on the faces of his audience, and added, 'I challenged Brown. He claimed to know nothing about it. Said he'd had a lot of his cows rustled, that maybe it was rustlers that altered the brands.'

'Did you believe him?' asked Dan.

'Hell no!' gnashed Jim. 'I wouldn't trust that polecat as far as I could throw an elephant.' He spat for extra emphasis. 'He's jealous, I guess.'

'Jealous?' asked Clem.

'Yep. He was desperate to get the government contract I got to supply beef to the Indian agent. I won it fair and square; he had his chance. Only trouble is he don't quite see things that way, thinks I only got it because of Ika. I know he broods about it. Hates the fact that he has to drive his herd to Kansas to sell 'em. Hates Indians. His ranch is like a fort. He ain't gonna like hearing about your deal to supply horses to the army neither. Talk is that he's agitatin' to get the railroad to

81

White Bluff. Heard it's cost him plenty so far.'

They rode as far as the western boundary of Jim's land, a fast-flowing river called Pitcher's Creek.

Jim pointed to the other side of the water. 'Always had a hankerin' fer that land.' He sniffed, broke a twig off an overhanging branch. 'Good grass, water all year round. Never got round to doin' anythin' about it, though.'

'Nobody owns it?'

'Nope. It's open range.' Jim adjusted his weight on his saddle and tossed the twig away. 'Brown would like it, but he can't get at it without trespassin' on land that belongs to me an' old Walter Schultz.'

'He could still buy it though, couldn't he?'

Jim shook his head. 'There's a rumour I've heard, that since the war ended, Brown's been having trouble raising money. I heard he made a couple of bad investments. Heard he had to borrow some to buy out a couple of the farmers,' Jim sniffed, 'and last year he lost a lot of cattle, water hole poisoned, somethin' like that. Miracle the other ranchers' cattle weren't affected.'

'Did you lose any?'

'No, sir. Lucky, I guess,' Jim answered.

'Brown sounds like a man that needs watchin'.'

'He's a tricky son-of-a-bitch, that's for sure,' said Jim.

* * *

Cheng Li placed a huge dish of fried chicken on the table, then brought fried potatoes, sweetcorn and biscuits.

'Tuck in, boys,' invited Jim Jackson. No one needed telling twice.

After the meal, Jeff asked, 'Uncle Jim. You promised to tell us something about your father.'

Jim Jackson smiled broadly. He was getting used to being addressed as uncle; he found he loved it. 'Well, now, let's see. Seems like my pa was a bit of a maverick; a bit too wild-natured for the polite society back east. Left home when I was still a kid, heading west to seek his fortune. I heard tell he joined up with a pair of Frenchies, trapping beaver and silver fox. A feller I met once told me that he'd married a Cheyenne Injun woman; lived with them for a time before taking a job scouting for them government survey-ors who found the passage through the Rockies. He never wrote.' A sadness appeared in Jim's eyes. 'After my mother died I was sent to live with your grandpa and grandma till I was in my late teens. Then I too got the wanderlust; guess it's in my blood. And, well, you know the rest.'

'Did you ever meet him?' Dan asked.

'No. That's one of my big regrets.' He sighed. 'Looked for him. Found people in frontier settlements who'd heard of him, plus a few who claimed to have known him, but never caught up with him. Heck, he might still be alive, with a great long white beard.' Jim chortled, leaning forward to rub Dan's head with his knuckles.

'Where was it you won your spread?' Clem piped up.

'Can't rightly say because the place didn't have a proper name,' Jim chuckled. 'It was in the gold fields, way up north. In a tent, we were. A kind of open-air saloon, playing stud poker. This old miner waltzes in and asks if he can sit in, said he had money. We said OK. That guy was the worst poker player I ever did see; he lost a packet.' Jim slapped his thigh to emphasize the point. 'When his cash ran out, he brought out a poke of gold; good size it was. We took most of it off him as well, the old galoot didn't seem to mind. The last hand of the night, which he insisted on, incidentally, saw me and him the only two left, big pot. I pushed my bet onto the pile, an' he looks at his hand, shuffles the five cards then puts them down, looks at 'em again then ferrets around in his pants and pulls out this stained piece of paper, said it was the deeds to a ranch, must be worth more than fifty dollars, he said. I took a look at it, seemed legit, and tossed it onto the pile. Then he eyed me carefully, and called me. Well, sir, he laid down his cards, face up, two pair, he said, aces and eights.' Jim suppressed a chuckle. 'The old-timer stretched out his gnarled hands towards the pot, I told him to hold his horses then laid down mine. 'Three little ladies,' I said, 'on top of two little deuces.' He didn't say anything other than 'What's your name?' I told him, and he wrote it on the paper, signing over the title to me, pushed back his chair with the backs of his legs and breezed out into the night. His name was Valentine Eugene Astor. Never saw him again. Folks were a-slapping me on the back, and cheering wildly. I bought them all a round of drinks and headed for the nearest lawyer, figurin' it best to get well clear of that place in case somebody decided they should have the money I had won. Had to ride me over a hundred miles before I found one. The transfer of deeds was recorded, an' here I am.'

Jim obviously loved telling the story. Jeff had to admit it was a beaut.

Jim went silent for a moment, obviously considering something. 'Technically,' he said, 'I guess you three own a good-sized chunk of this spread.'

'How come?' Jeff asked.

'Well, as I see it, my pa was staked by your granddaddy when he left home. An' they looked after me when I needed it. If it weren't for them I'd have never had the sand to do what I done. I was lucky and ended up with this ranch, so I'd say my part of the family owes your part. Namely, a piece of this ranch. In any case, I got no kids that made it, so you three are the only legit kin I got.'

'Surely that can't be right, Uncle Jim?'

'Whether tis or t'ain't makes never-no-mind, 'cause when I finally kick the bucket I'm leavin' her to you three. Always planned it that way, leavin' it to

Joe and Archie's families, I mean.' Clem was about to lead the protests when Jim held up both hands. 'I ain't hearing any negativities. My mind's made up. Any case, I want you to have it. Who else have I got to leave it to?'

'What about Ika and the kids?'

'Ain't what you'd call legally married. Any case, Indians can't own land, not in a white man kind of way.' Jim held up a hand. 'I love 'em to bits, but they can't inherit. So when I'm gone the Double-J is yours. I already talked it over with Ika, and she agrees.' Jim lit a pipe. 'Anyway, now it's your turn. So you served in the war?' All three nodded. 'Union Army, I hope.'

'Yep,' Clem replied. 'Jeff was an exalted officer. Captain, no less. Me and Dan were lowly sergeants. Dan looked after the horses, I looked after Jeff,' he chuckled.

Dan piped up. 'Took me a while to start calling him sir, I can tell you.' He motioned to where Jeff sat. 'Never really got used to it,' he grinned.

Jeff turned. 'That'll be enough, sergeant,' he joked.

'See?' said Dan. 'That's the kind of thing I had to put up with throughout the war.'

'You're lucky,' sniped Clem. 'I've had to put up with it all my life.'

★ ★ ★

After breakfast next morning Jeff spoke to Jim.

'Uncle Jim, mind if I ask you something?'

'Sure thing, Jeff. Anything. What is it?'

'Well, me and the boys were talking about what you said last night about deciding to leave the ranch to us.'

'Don't you boys start thinkin' I didn't mean what I said. I meant it all right. Fact is I've already written it down. My last will and testament. Sanchez and Cheng Li have witnessed it.'

'No. It's not that. Well, not exactly.

We never doubted your sincerity, and we are all very grateful, and honoured that you would think of doing such a thing. Let's put that to one side for a moment. I wanted to ask about that land bordering your spread you showed us. Fact is, me and the boys would like to buy some of it.'

'That's a great idea, Jeff. What about money?' Jim grinned. 'I can let you have — '

'We got money,' Jeff said, shaking his head. 'Had some luck in the war, and we'll pool our army pay. So, do you know for sure if anyone owns the land?'

'As far I as I'm concerned the land west of here is open range. South is the Flying B, Zeb Bone's place. Walter Schultz's Bar S lies north, Brown's spread north of that. Only canyons and mountains to the east.'

Jeff wanted to be certain. 'You're sure you have no objections to us buying it?'

'No. Not a one.' Jim reached over and patted Jeff on the back. 'Love you to,' he grinned.

In what seemed no time at all, the deal was done. Jeff had written to the government's territorial land agent, paperwork had been exchanged, documents signed and processed. The boys now owned a sizeable chunk of Montana territory.

Billy looked disinterested until Jeff told him to come to the table and take a look.

'One quarter of this is yours,' Jeff announced. Clem and Dan grinned at Billy's expression of amazement.

'W . . . what?'

'You didn't think we'd leave you out, did you?'

Billy's eyes misted over as he realized what was being said. 'But, I ain't got no money,' he protested emotionally, looking around at the three smiling faces.

'All taken care of,' said Jeff. 'You've earned it.'

Jeff's words proved to be the straw

that broke the camel's back; floods of tears gushed from Billy's eyes. He hugged each in turn. Jeff saw Clem wipe away a tear, as he did the same.

7

Jim Jackson strode purposely across the yard like a parade-ground sergeant. 'Boys, Cheng Li's burned his hand, so he can't drive the wagon, and my cowboys are out workin'.' He didn't need to add 'unlike you pair of . . . ' They had already taken his meaning. 'I need a volunteer to go into town for some supplies. Any takers?'

Clem and Dan, who were sitting on the corral fence, squirmed around, obviously not interested in volunteering for anything.

Jeff emerged from the barn. 'I'll go,' he called out, 'I've a hankering to see White Bluff for myself.' He hadn't yet been to town. Jeff shot Clem and Dan a dirty look. 'You two can hitch up the wagon, 'stead of sitting there wearing out the seat of your pants.'

To Clem and Dan this was déjà vu,

like being back in the army. Dan almost saluted.

'Thanks, Jeff,' said Jim. 'Cheng Li has made a list of vitals and supplies; he's in the kitchen. Feel free to add a few comforts for yourself if you want.'

'Right you are.' Jeff wandered off to the kitchen to see Cheng Li. Clem and Dan went to organize the wagon.

★　★　★

Jeff drew up the wagon outside the general store, wiped his forehead on his sleeve, climbed down from the seat, secured the team and stepped up onto the boardwalk.

The door of White Bluff's general store swung open a split second before Jeff could turn the handle; the doorbell tinkled brightly. He stepped back and removed his hat as two chattering, gingham-clad women stood in the doorway facing him.

Jeff smiled. 'Ladies.'

'Good morning, young man,' said

one as they walked past the tall, handsome stranger; the other returned Jeff's smile coyly.

Jeff heard them giggling, girl-like, as they continued along the boardwalk. He chuckled inwardly, put on his hat and entered the store, closing the glass-centred door behind him as quietly as the doorbell would allow. It was refreshingly cool inside in comparison to the stifling heat outside.

Tiny dust particles floated gently in the still air. Jeff scanned the well-polished counter; no one seemed to be in attendance. His eyes lighted on a line of glass jars filled with colourful candy.

'Morning, stranger. What can I do for you?'

The female voice, although soothing, startled Jeff. A young woman emerged from behind a pile of wooden boxes at the side of the counter. Sunlight streamed through the big store windows, highlighting the colour of her corn-yellow hair, worn long against the fashion of the day. Jeff was instantly taken aback by her handsome features. He thought her the loveliest girl he had ever seen; her proud bearing and high cheekbones, forced higher by her natural even-toothed smile, made a stunningly attractive picture. Hers was a pleasing, open face, oval-shaped with bright blue eyes that sparkled mischievously either side of a nose that he was sure had been broken at least once. Her tanned skin seemed to shine. Her movement was graceful. Jeff found himself entranced. He noticed her finely shaped hands and long slender fingers, absent of rings, as she placed them gently on the polished oak countertop. He was about to remove his hat when her full mouth, wide and sensuous, opened.

'Cowboy!' Her voice went up a decibel, snapping Jeff from his thoughtful examination.

'What?'

'I asked what you wanted.'

Jeff took off his hat. 'Sorry, ma'am.'

'Miss,' she corrected. 'Andersen,' she added, holding out her right hand in his direction.

Jeff fumbled with the glove on his right hand, eventually getting it off, but dropping it on the floor with a dull thud. He smoothed his palm against his thigh then took her hand and shook it. Her skin was smoother than he imagined, and warm.

'Pleased to make your acquaintance, Miss Andersen.'

She smiled.

'Jeff Jackson.' He smiled back, still holding on to her hand. 'My uncle owns the Double-J ranch.'

'Oh!' she exclaimed in a half-whispered voice. 'Your uncle?'

Jeff nodded. 'Yes, ma'am. I mean, Miss Andersen.'

She smiled again, her expression full of mischievousness. 'Call me Laurie, everybody does, and I'll call you Jeff. OK?'

'Fine with me,' replied Jeff.

Laurie examined the face of the tall

young man. 'Now, Jeff, what can I do for you?'

Jeff dug out the list from inside his left glove, unfolded the piece of paper and smoothed it out on the counter-top. Laurie turned the list to face her, scanning the neat pencil writing.

'I'm sure we have everything on your list.' The doorbell tinkled prettily. Laurie looked up at the lady who had entered; Jeff turned to see who it was. 'Be with you in a moment, Mrs Morgan,' Laurie said politely. She turned back to Jeff. 'Your order will take a little while to fill. That OK?' Jeff nodded. 'Where shall I have the items put?' she asked.

'Wagon's right outside the store, miss, sorry, Laurie,' he corrected, a little embarrassed to say her Christian name. 'Horses are branded Double-J. Can't really miss it.'

'You going to wait?' she asked.

'No, I have a few other chores. All right if I come back in thirty minutes?'

'Make it an hour.' She looked up into

his face. 'If that's all right.'

Jeff put on his hat, tipped it. 'Fine, Laurie,' he said, turning toward the door. 'Ma'am,' he said to the lady who had come in. She looked up from the bolts of material she had been looking through.

The doorbell tinkled as the door closed. 'What a nice young man,' the woman said to Laurie. 'Handsome too.' She had a twinkle in her eye.

'Jeff Jackson,' Laurie told her, 'Jim Jackson's nephew. New in town.'

* * *

It started to rain as Jeff crossed the street. He leaped onto the boardwalk, took off his hat and shook off the water, then crammed it back on his head. Two men were walking purposely in his direction, the dull clump of their boots on the wooden boards accompanied by the jingle of spurs. One, taller than average, was dressed from head to foot in black. The other, stockier, and shorter by half a foot, wore a short sheepskin jacket and denims. Lank, greasy hair jutted out from beneath a battered and stained Stetson that was pulled forward, hiding most of his unshaven face. The tall man, slim and long-striding, wore a pair of pearl-handled six-guns low on his hips. A thin silver hatband sparkled brightly even in the dull daylight. The man's steely eyes were hooded, his expression a picture of concentration.

Jeff eyed the pair warily. If he'd had any sense he would surely have stepped back onto the rutted roadway, but Jeff was never one to step aside. As the men neared, Jeff tensed his muscles, expecting the worst, hoping for the best. The boardwalk was wide enough to accommodate only two people; Jeff decided to make directly for the shorter man.

Two steps from convergence, the stocky cowboy dropped back a pace behind. Instinctively Jeff allowed his guard to fall. He was about to say thanks when the tall man veered, his shoulder deliberately barging Jeff's.

Jeff lurched against a roof support, immediately righting his body, not sure how to react. The cowboy in black made up his mind for him.

Thin lips drew back in a vengeful snarl. 'Watch where you're going,' the cowboy spat out.

Common sense suggested to Jeff that he should ignore what had just happened. However, Jeff Jackson had never backed away from a fight, regardless of the odds. He weighed up the situation in an instant.

Jeff's blurred right fist shot upwards with the unexpected speed of a cobra strike, catching Ray Cole smack on the point of his jaw; the blow sounded like a hammer striking a log. The man's eyes came together as his head was whipped backwards by the force of the blow; the soles of his boots lifted a fraction off the boardwalk before his body crashed down onto the timber surface with an almighty bang.

Before the other cowboy could react,

Jeff had pulled the stocky man's six-gun from its holster with his left hand.

'Back up,' Jeff commanded.

Whitey Bell looked down at his cohort's prone body. His hands shot up above his head, knocking off his soiled Stetson. 'Hold on, stranger,' he pleaded in a squeaky voice.

'Grab your friend's six-guns, and toss them over here.' Jeff's cold-eyed order was clear. The cowboy did as he was told. Jeff pushed the tall cowboy's guns into his belt. 'Where's the sheriff's office?'

The cowboy nodded his head. 'Along the boardwalk. Past the saloon.'

'Young man!' Jeff turned his head to face the shout.

A middle-aged woman carrying a large wicker basket called out. 'I saw everything. That oaf asked for what he got. I'll come with you to the sheriff's office.'

'Thank you, ma'am. I'm much obliged.'

'You.' Jeff poked the gun into the

stocky cowboy's midriff. 'Pick him up.'

It was a struggle, but they made it. The woman opened the lawman's door, preceding the small procession into the jailhouse.

'Sheriff!' she called out in a loud voice. 'You need to lock up these two ruffians.' For a split second the sheriff's mouth hung open, then relaxed.

'What?' he said, his voice deep and gruff.

The woman spoke before Jeff could answer. 'I want you to lock up these two ruffians.'

Ethan Todd eyed Jeff and his two prisoners.

'On what charge?' he drawled.

'Assault and battery,' the woman cried out. 'I saw it all, Sheriff. I am your witness.'

'What'd they do?' Todd drew in another lungful of satisfaction.

Again she was in before Jeff could speak. 'They ganged up on this young man. Forced him to protect himself.'

'Can I put Ray down?' the shorter of

the two cowboys asked. Jeff nodded, as the still unconscious body slumped to the floor.

'Appears to me like they're the ones need protectin'.' The sheriff's slow and sarcastic tone was beginning to grate on Jeff. 'You knock him out?' He addressed the question to Jeff, pointing to the prone cowboy.

'I wasn't looking for any trouble, Sheriff.'

'No. But you found some right enough.' The sheriff took a sheet of paper from the top drawer of his desk. 'Tell me exactly what happened.' He held up his hand to stay the woman. 'You'll get your turn, Mrs Bergmann.'

Jeff told what had happened. The sheriff laboriously wrote it down in a none too neat hand, repeating the process with Mrs Bergmann.

'I'll lock 'em up fer now and speak to Judge Lowe.' He lifted a large bunch of keys from a hook on the wall, unlocked a door and herded the two cowboys inside, the shorter man still having to half-carry his amigo. The sheriff looked back at Jeff and Mrs Bergmann. 'That's all. Close the door on your way out.'

The icy water splashed across the cell into Ray Cole's swarthy face.

'Hey, watch it,' Whitey protested.

Sheriff Todd ignored the protest and slapped Cole's cheeks. 'Wakey, wakey,' he said sarcastically.

Ray Cole came round with a splutter. He tried to get to his feet but toppled over.

'Get 'im up,' Todd ordered.

Whitey Bell brushed an imaginary drop of water from his sheepskin jacket, and tugged his partner to his unsteady feet.

Todd was mad. 'Aw, sit 'im down!' he shouted.

Bell leaned his cohort against the cell bars and, with an outstretched leg, slid a stool under him.

Sheriff Todd patted Cole's cheek again. 'C'mon, Ray.' But Ray Cole was not yet ready for consciousness. The sheriff turned on Whitey Bell. 'Well?'

Bell stammered out an embarrassed explanation. 'Ray said, 'Let's have some fun with this feller' an' barged into 'im. Boy, was that guy fast. Before I could do anything the stranger flattened Ray with one punch, grabbed my six-gun and got the drop on me.'

'An' you just stood there?'

Whitey looked more sheepish than his jacket. 'I couldn't'a done nothin', Ethan, the guy was too fast.'

'You're lucky he didn't plug the both of you useless bastards.'

'Weren't doing anythin', just havin' a little fun.'

'Brown's orders are to keep a low profile when you're in town. Don't you ever listen?' Todd shouted. 'Soon as he comes back to the land of the living, get him out to the Circle B.'

'OK, Ethan.'

'Tell Cole to stay out of town, and to keep well away from Jim Jackson's boys.'

An hour later Ray Cole told his stocky comrade, 'I'm gonna get that son-of-a-bitch fer what he done.'

'Now, Ray, remember what Ethan said,' cautioned Whitey.

'I don't give a rat's ass for Todd's opinion.' Cole fingered the scar on his cheek. 'He ain't my boss. I'll see that bastard dead before I'm through,' he threatened.

* * *

His business completed, Jeff walked back to the general store, passing the wagon which he was pleased to see had been loaded. The doorbell tinkled as he entered.

Laurie Andersen looked up from the ledger, and set down her pen. 'Hello again, Jeff Jackson.' Her smile was captivating. 'Your supplies are all loaded, all but a couple of items that were out of stock. Should be here in a day or so. Here's the reckoning.' She pushed a stiff piece of paper across the counter. 'Let's go through it.'

To Jeff, her voice was like a trickle of

velvety honey. In his dreamlike trance Jeff heard every word as she ticked off each item, but at no time could he tell anyone what they were. He was genuinely smitten.

'Jeff. Jeff!' Laurie called out. Jeff's glazed expression snapped back to reality. He looked where Laurie was pointing. 'This is my father,' she announced.

The stocky man with the drooping moustache clapped him on the shoulder. 'Pleased to meet you,' he said, his accent unmistakably Scandinavian.

Jeff drew himself to his full height and took the hand the man held out.

'Pleased to meet you, Mr . . . ' Jeff paused.

'Andersen,' the man said, 'Lars Andersen.'

The doorbell tinkled to announce a new caller.

'Morning, Mrs Bergmann,' Laurie and Lars Andersen chorused.

Jeff turned at the mention of the name and offered a greeting.

Mrs Bergmann's face and throat flushed when she saw who was standing at the counter. Her mouth opened to return the greeting but no words came out. Recovering from her momentary attack of the vapours she managed to speak, albeit with a voice that held a degree of shakiness.

'Morning, all.' She reserved a special greeting for Jeff. 'Nice to see you again so soon, young man.'

Jeff saw Laurie and her father exchange curious looks.

'We met earlier,' he said.

Mrs Bergmann found a stronger voice. 'Laurie, this young man is a hero.'

Jeff coloured; Laurie was intrigued.

Mrs Bergmann sighed deeply and placed a gloved hand on her chest before taking a deep breath. 'Two of Alexander Brown's ruffians. Out there on the boardwalk.' She pointed towards the door. Her words were uttered in staccato style. 'He was magnificent. At last we have a real man in town.' Jeff blushed bright red as Mrs Bergmann continued her verbal hero worship. 'Now at last we can feel safe in our own beds.' Her speech delivered, Mrs Bergmann flopped onto a chair, dabbing her face with a handkerchief she took from her sleeve.

Laurie almost laughed when she saw how Jeff was squirming. 'We heard a commotion, didn't we, Father?' Lars nodded. 'Wondered what it was.'

Jeff didn't say anything, but Mrs Bergmann did. 'Sheriff Todd has them in jail under lock and key.'

Lars butted in. 'Well, you can bet your bottom dollar they'll be out before sunset.'

'How so?' Jeff asked, removing his hat.

'Brown owns the sheriff. His men do whatever they like in this town,' Laurie explained. 'He's got an army of gunmen out at his ranch.' Lars was still tut-tutting as he returned to the stockroom.

Out of the blue, Mrs Bergmann

asked, 'Laurie, are you going to the dance on Saturday?'

Jeff's ears pricked up.

'I haven't decided.'

'Whyever not? A young girl like you *should* attend.'

'Oh, I don't know, Mrs Bergmann.' There was a sadness in Laurie's voice. 'The last one was a disaster once those Circle B cowboys arrived.'

Laurie's comment rekindled Mrs Bergmann's memory. 'Ooh, you're right, Laurie. It was awful.' She held her handkerchief to her nose, but didn't blow. 'The way that young cowboy was gunned down was horrible.'

'The killer got away scot-free. Claimed it was a fair fight, but it was nothing short of murder. Sheriff Todd did nothing.'

'What do you expect? They are both in the pay of that Scottish tyrant. The poor lad never stood a chance.' Mrs Bergmann handed over the money to pay her bill, and smiled benignly. 'Well, perhaps you'll change your mind. I'll hope to see you there. Goodbye.'

'Goodbye,' Laurie called out. Mrs Bergmann waved from the open doorway, nodded her head towards Jeff, whose back was turned. Laurie recognized the encouragement and returned Mrs Bergmann's smile.

The doorbell tinkled as Mrs Bergmann opened and closed the door.

Jeff had heard what had been said; an opportunity was there for the taking. He took in a deep breath of air, crossed his fingers and went for it.

'Laurie,' he said as sweetly as he could, 'I heard what you told Mrs Bergmann about not going to the dance.' Before she could respond Jeff added, 'I would be mighty honoured if you would allow me to escort you.'

Laurie's eyes flashed with surprise. She had liked Jeff immediately, hoped that a friendship might develop between them, but this? This was too soon — wasn't it?

Uncertain of how to react, she chose the time-honoured fashion of defence.

'But I hardly know you.'

Jeff pondered her words. 'Hmm?' He leaned forward, resting one elbow on the counter. 'Seems to me that might be a good way to get to know each other.' His smile grew wider. 'What do you say?'

Lars came back in before his daughter could think of an answer. 'What's that, young feller?' he asked.

'I was just asking your daughter if I could escort her to the dance.'

'Oh.' Lars realized he'd poked his nose into something best left to these two people to resolve; however, he couldn't resist helping. 'What was her answer?'

'Father!' yelled Laurie, feigning indignation. 'I am here, you know!'

To Jeff, Lars said, 'Ask her again.'

Jeff accepted the challenge. 'Well, Miss Andersen? Will you come?'

Laurie looked into Jeff's brown eyes; he was handsome and seemed nice. She looked at her father, who smiled encouragement, then back to Jeff.

'OK. I'll come.'

Lars chuckled and returned to the back room.

'That's settled, then. Pick you up at . . . ' he hesitated, 'what time?'

'Around six. Earlier if you want.'

* * *

Late Saturday afternoon Jeff rode into White Bluff; he was a little late. Jeff left his horse at the livery stable and walked to Laurie's. He was wearing a dark-grey jacket he'd borrowed from his uncle, hoping it was appropriate and that Laurie would approve. He left his gun rig with the hostler, who had locked it inside a cupboard.

The Andersens' house was at the end of a dark alley adjoining the side of the store.

There was a chill in the air as fall moved closer to winter. When Jeff stepped into the narrow alleyway, his heart almost stopped. Laurie stood framed in the open doorway, her slender figure accentuated by the lamplight behind her, her blonde hair silhouetted against a halo of light. Jeff recalled how lovely she was. Never before had he held such feelings for a girl. Seeing her framed by the lamplight kindled all kinds of urges he hadn't felt for a long time.

'There you are. I was beginning to think you had changed your mind,' she said softly.

He was standing but a couple of paces away from her, not remembering walking the twenty-or-so steps along the alley. For a moment Jeff was tongue-tied then managed to mutter out, 'Sorry I'm late.'

Laurie smiled radiantly. 'Come in,' she said. She stepped to one side and gestured with a hand.

Jeff took off his hat, instinctively slapping it against his thigh. He was unsure how to greet her: should he shake her hand, bow, kiss her? What?

Laurie made up his mind for him; stretching up onto tiptoe, she kissed him on the cheek.

Jeff enjoyed the dance and the refreshments. He enjoyed meeting the many people Laurie introduced him to. Most of all, he enjoyed being with her, constantly praying that the musicians would play another waltz so he could hold her tightly to him, feel the warmth of her body against his, breathe in the soap-fresh scent of her golden hair as they spun around the dance floor, wishing that this night could last for ever. He was falling in love with Laurie Andersen faster than he ever imagined.

The event was a success with not one ounce of trouble — due entirely to the fact that none of the Circle B riders attended.

After a cup of coffee with Laurie's father, Jeff took his leave, promising to see her again very soon.

The passionate kisses they had shared lingered on his lips all the way home.

8

White Bluff

Their business at the bank completed, the brothers stepped into the street. The warm sun felt good on their faces.

'Let's get something to eat before we pick up the rest of them supplies. I could bust half a steer between two slices of bread.' Clem was starving after a shift riding night-hawk on Jim's cattle.

'OK,' said Jeff, following his brother to Mrs O'Shaughnessy's eating parlour.

Bellies full, Clem suggested a quick drink. Jeff agreed, but reminded Clem he would be off to see Laurie after one beer.

The saloon was almost empty. A couple of cowboys lounged at a table near the door. Clem ordered two beers.

Jeff nudged Clem as the batwing doors banged open with a loud crack.

A lanky, baby-faced young cowboy with dirty-blond, almost white, hair stood motionless, holding the doors open as if to make sure everyone in the saloon knew he had arrived. Jeff immediately noticed his wild eyes — mad-dog eyes. The newcomer stood in the doorway for some time, a false grin on his weasel-like face. With a flourish he relaxed his grip on the doors, the batwings clattered together. He pushed the wide-brimmed hat to the back of his head and peered around, blinking through a straggly fringe of hair which he blew out of his eyes.

His face was long and thin, his eyes close-set. A weird, forced smile, a crazy, mangled effort through a mouthful of crooked and discoloured teeth, spread across his face.

His dusty, long black coat had seen better times and was at least two sizes too big for him. His baggy trousers were worn tucked into his poor-man boots. A pair of Colt .45s, butt forward, were tied down low on his hips in a cross-belt rig. He looked like trouble with a capital T.

His left eye twitched minutely as his thin lips opened a fraction.

'Evenin', gents,' he drawled as he ambled to the bar, his accent deep south.

Most, including Jeff and Clem, turned away, believing the short show marking the newcomer's comedic entrance was over. A couple of cowboys took a second glance before returning unimpressed to their drinks and momentarily interrupted conversations.

Undeterred, the newcomer leaned the backs of his elbows on the bar.

Hooking one heel over the brass rail he surveyed the bar room then spoke again, his voice much louder now. 'I'm the Lafayette Kid. You've probably heard of me.' His words were more a statement than a question, his tone daring anyone to challenge him.

A deathly hush descended over the saloon.

'That kid's hunting trouble,' commented Clem. 'Looks like he wants some real bad.'

The Kid's eyes took in every expression on the faces looking at him. 'I'm lookin' fer Alexander Brown.'

The barkeep relaxed his grip on the shotgun kept out of sight under the bar. 'Brown ain't in town today,' he volunteered. 'Best try his ranch, Circle B.'

'Gimme a shot of whiskey,' the Kid ordered, turning to face the bar. When the barman hesitated, the Kid pushed back one fold of his coat. 'You aimin' to use that shotgun?'

The bartender's eyes filled with fear, wondering how the Kid knew about the concealed shotgun. He forced a thin smile, his hands appearing holding a bottle and a shot-glass. He poured, his hand trembling noticeably. Whiskey spilled over the polished surface of the bar.

'Look what you're doin', you clumsy ape.'

The barkeep mopped the spillage with a cloth. The Kid swallowed the whiskey in one gulp. 'Hit me agin,' he ordered. The barkeep did as he was told. The Kid gulped down the fiery liquid and wiped a sleeve across his mouth. 'Tell me how to get to Brown's spread.'

The bartender ran through the directions twice.

The Kid turned to walk away.

The bartender coughed. 'Excuse me, sir,' he said nervously.

The Kid swivelled; there was no smile now. The barkeep extended an open hand towards the Kid, but before he could speak the Kid told him, 'Put it on Brown's tab. I'm his new ramrod.' The Kid turned on his heel and strode purposely out of the saloon.

'Let's get the supplies,' said Jeff.

The brothers ambled to the general store, unconcerned about the arrival of Brown's new gunhand.

Lars Andersen filled their order, and Clem drove the wagon back to the ranch, leaving Jeff at the store to await Laurie's return.

Back at the Double-J, Clem described the arrival of the Lafayette Kid, then went to get some well-deserved sleep before he and Dan set off at first light to catch some mustangs.

★   ★   ★

Dan and Clem had worked hard all morning and decided to take a well-earned rest and brew up some coffee and food. The fourteen mustangs they had caught milled around behind the fence poles at the mouth of the finger canyon, protesting loudly at their incarceration. The second cup of coffee went down as sweet as the first. The sun was high in the clear sky, the air still and clean.

Still tired from the previous night, Clem announced he was going to catch forty winks. He pulled his Stetson over his eyes and settled the nape of his neck against the blanket he'd draped across a fallen log.

'Howdy, boys.' The caller was a big, broad-shouldered bear of a man, looked to be in his early fifties. A black ten-gallon was pushed way back on his head, revealing a weather-beaten face. He was alone — or appeared to be.

The loud, deep voice snapped Clem out of his nap. He looked around, feeling the presence of others concealed from view.

'Mind telling me where you got them horses?' The man had a long scar on his forehead and was missing a couple of teeth, which gave him a fearsome countenance.

Dan touched Clem's arm. 'They're wild horses, Mister. We rounded them up ourselves.' Clem sensed trouble brewing. 'Is there a problem?'

'Might be,' the man drawled, his accent foreign. 'I think you'll find them horses belong to me.'

'No, mister, they're ours. We caught 'em fair and square.'

'Horse stealin's a serious offence in

these parts. Horse thieves usually get themselves hung.'

Clem drew himself up to his full height, resting a hand on his Colt. 'There's no brand on 'em, mister.'

'Makes no mind, son. If you got 'em anywhere within fifty miles of here, they're mine. Belong to me an' that's a fact.'

'How come?' Dan asked.

''Cause I own this land, laddie. That's how come. This ain't open range.' The man waved his arm, gesturing to the horizon. 'Yes, sir. As far as you can see, an' then some, I own it. *All* of it,' he emphasized. 'Settled it, fought off jay-hawkers and Indians, lost a wife and two sons; my family's blood is soaked into this land.'

Clem wasn't about to be pushed around. 'No offence, mister, but you're wrong. We got papers on this land from the government, all legal and above board. So, we got a right to catch wild horses, run cattle, anything we want.' The man was about to butt in but Clem didn't allow it. 'What is more, we got a contract with the army to provide cavalry mounts.' The man's face twitched. 'Furthermore, actually, mister, you're trespassing on *our* land.'

'That a fact?' the big man growled.

'Sure is.'

'You from the Double-J?' the man demanded.

'Yes. Jim Jackson's nephews,' shouted Dan. 'What of it?'

'Jimmy Jackson, eh?' The man pondered. 'That low-down skunk is a no-good squatter.'

'Mister, aside from being inaccurate, that's a downright insult, which I do not take kindly to. So I'd be obliged if you'd get down off that horse.'

The man moved his right hand away from his side arm. 'I'm not looking for a fight today, sonny, but I'll be payin' you folks another call real soon. In the meantime you'd best take heed of my words. Get off my land and stay off.'

With that he wrenched on his reins and spurred his big roan horse into a gallop, leaving a haze of dust in his wake.

'Bastard!' Dan called out.

'Good description,' agreed Clem. 'I'm sure we haven't seen the last of him.'

'Wonder who he was?'

'I'd say we just met Alexander Brown himself.' Clem watched the remnants of the small dust cloud disappear from view. 'Let's get these horses back to the corral. Jeff will want to know about this.'

'Looks like we had better check those deeds,' said Dan ruefully.

The sound of the horse galloping away was soon joined by the pounding of other hoofs. Clem knew he hadn't been mistaken.

As Clem predicted, Jeff was madder than a wildcat at what Clem told him.

'We better ride over to Gallatin City and sort this out.'

'That's more than a fifty-mile ride,' said Clem.

'Then we better make a start,' Jeff grimaced.

'It'll be dark soon,' Clem said questioningly.

Jeff shot back an answer. 'We'll camp out on the range. That way we'll get there early in the morning.'

9

Gallatin City, Montana Territory

'Can't say how, boys, but that parcel of land seems to have been omitted from your deeds.' The land agent pushed the small round spectacles further up his nose.

Jeff slapped the edge of the agent's desk, his head filled with negative thoughts. The agent's matter-of-fact attitude wasn't helping much. 'Now, you just hold on a minute, mister. You saying we don't have title to that land?'

'Appears not. Sorry.' The agent sniffed. 'And please do not raise your voice.'

'Can't be right,' Jeff sighed, tracing a line across the parchment map spread out in front of them with his finger. The agent looked at him blankly. Jeff slammed his other hand on the desk. 'Look, there's our boundary line.'

The agent bent his head forward. 'No. Sorry,' he sniffed. 'Seems there's a mistake on your map and title documents.'

Jeff shook his head. 'What do you mean? It's as clear as day.'

The agent slipped a smaller map onto the table. 'See this,' he pointed. 'The section you are talking about, this one here,' he prodded a section marked in red with a stubby finger, 'this is the land you are disputing.' He looked up. 'Correct?' Both nodded. 'This was the subject of an earlier transaction. That section belongs to another party. There. Look! Your boundary line stops several miles from the foothills.'

Jeff was not convinced. 'But our documents came from this office; how can there have been a mistake?'

'Did you make the transaction in person?'

'No, by post.'

'Oh, no. That won't do. That will be where the error was made.' His all-knowing expression was conde-scending. 'By you,' he added.

'Look. Where's the agent that dealt with our purchase?' demanded Jeff.

'As I thought I had already explained, Mr Jackson, I am the land agent, the only one operating from this office.'

Jeff's frustration threatened to boil over into something more serious. Clem laid a steadying hand on his brother's arm. Jeff nodded to reassure his brother that he had understood.

'May we see your copy of the deeds?' Clem enquired politely.

The agent stiffened. 'I'm afraid that is out of the question.' The agent saw Jeff's expression harden. 'They are private documents,' he added swiftly. 'In any case they are not kept here.'

'Where *are* they kept?' Jeff snapped.

The agent hesitated visibly. He was a man of noticeably nervous disposition when put under pressure.

'Tell us!' Jeff's loud demand echoed across the office, forcing a nervous response.

'O-our attorney, Lawyer McCall, holds all our documents.' The agent stuttered out the words, suddenly wary of the two men facing him.

'This is bullshit!' yelled Jeff. 'Who is this owner?'

The agent pulled himself together. 'I refuse to be intimidated like this.'

'Sorry,' apologized Clem. 'Please will you tell us the name of the person you say is the rightful owner?'

'I'm afraid that's also confidential. And in any case, Mr Brown — ' The agent pulled up short then attempted to retrace his verbal mistake. 'The owner,' he corrected, 'has applied to purchase the adjoining foothills.'

'Are you saying Alexander Brown is the owner?' demanded Jeff.

The agent's reddened face twitched. 'No. I . . . er, I'm not saying that. It was merely a simple mistake. A slip of the tongue.'

'So that's the game,' Jeff retorted, his face like thunder.

Clem grabbed his brother's arm.

'Let's go get a drink and something to eat.' To the agent he said sharply, 'We'll be back in one hour. Make sure you have all the correctly dated documentation here. We *will* want to see it.'

Jeff's head was spinning with guilt and disbelief; he'd been the one the others had trusted to make the purchase. Until a few moments ago he was sure he had done everything correctly. He made no protest as Clem guided him out into the street.

Clem leaned against a roof support, his back towards the street. 'Well, what do you reckon?'

Jeff eyed his brother, suddenly calm. 'Clem, where we come from they call it a swindle. No other word for it.'

Clem nodded. 'But why? That's what I don't understand.'

Jeff was pondering the situation when a large man bumped into him.

'Sorry, friend.' The gruff apology had more than a trace of a Scottish accent.

The man hurried away, a second man

almost having to run to keep up with the big man's long stride.

Clem grabbed his brother's arm. 'Jeff. That was Alexander Brown. I'd recognize that voice anywhere.'

'Who's the other feller?'

'Dunno, never seen him before, but from the look of his clothing I'd say he's a miner, or prospector, something like that. Either way I've a mind to see what he's up to.' The brothers followed at a distance.

Clem pointed to three men standing in the shadows on the other side of the street; Brown appeared to be making a bee line for them. The five men greeted each other and walked along the sunlit boardwalk.

Clem touched his brother's arm. 'I'm certain that's Brown's ramrod, Red West, and look, that's Sheriff Todd. I think the other feller's the Lafayette Kid. Remember? The cowboy in the saloon?'

Jeff nodded. 'You're right, that's him.'

The five men climbed the outside

staircase of a tall, timber-framed building, entering a door at the top. The brothers ambled over, keeping under cover where they could. A large brass sign said Assay Office.

'Wonder what Brown's up to.'

Jeff and Clem returned to the sidewalk across the street and watched. They waited for the best part of an hour, but neither Brown nor any of those accompanying him came out. They were just about to leave when the door at the top of the stairs swung open. Red West emerged carrying a rolled-up parchment and loped down the steps.

'I'll see where he's headed. You stay here,' Jeff suggested.

Red didn't go far; he entered a building one block away. Jeff knew it well, he and Clem had just come from there — the Territory Land Office.

Jeff sneaked a peep through a window, and saw Red hand over the rolled-up parchment map. Jeff couldn't hear what was being said, but saw the agent smile and nod before stowing it in the safe. Red handed over a large package then left. Jeff stayed where he was. The agent undid the twine holding the package — the package contained banknotes.

The agent re-wrapped the package of money, put it in a carpetbag and slid the bag under his desk.

Jeff returned to where Clem was waiting. He told his brother what he had seen.

'Red's gone back up the stairs,' Clem told him. 'No one has come out.'

Jeff's brain was going at a pace, figuring out the best way to react. 'Let's go back to the Land Office and confront the agent.'

'Won't work,' said Clem, 'not without an independent witness.'

Jeff nodded. 'You're right. Let's get the local lawman.'

'No!' said Clem. 'Brown might be paying him as well.'

'What about a lawyer?' suggested Jeff. Clem agreed.

'Two lawyers in Gallatin,' the first person they stopped told them. 'There's Lawyer McCall. His office is a red-brick building on Main Street. Other's named Nagel.' The man pointed across the street. 'That's his office over there.'

'Nagel's closest,' Clem said.

Ernst Nagel agreed to see them right away. Their request seemed extraordinary when they asked him to accompany them to act as a witness, telling him they didn't want to say more for fear of prejudicing what the lawyer saw. Nagel told them his rate and followed the brothers to the Land Agency.

The agency door was locked. Jeff hammered on the door.

'I don't understand it. He was here just a moment ago.'

Lawyer Nagel took out his pocket watch. 'Hmm. It's unusual for the office to be closed this early. Perhaps Mr Simmons has stepped out for a moment,' he suggested.

Jeff made his way to the side of the

building and peered through the window he'd looked through earlier. The office was deserted. The agent's desk, previously cluttered, was now completely empty.

Lawyer Nagel's patience was wearing a bit thin. 'Mind telling me what you hoped I would witness?' he said.

'Can't,' retorted Jeff. 'Prejudice, remember?'

Nagel nodded. 'OK, how do you want to proceed?'

'We'll wait,' snapped Jeff. Clem touched his impatient brother's arm. 'Sorry,' Jeff muttered.

The weak sun began to disappear behind the western hills. In houses all around town oil lamps were being lit.

'I don't think he's coming back today,' said Clem.

Reluctantly Jeff took out some money and counted out a number of bills into Lawyer Nagel's hand. Nagel handed back two bills. 'I don't believe I've earned the full amount.' He smiled. 'You know where I am if you need my services again.' When neither Jeff or Clem answered, Nagel said, 'I'll bid you goodnight, then.' He turned on his heel with Jeff's and Clem's goodnight hanging in the air.

Jeff cursed loudly. 'Let's get that drink!'

Clem agreed. 'There's a saloon near the office where Brown and his buckaroos are.'

No lights were showing in the assay office either. Jeff cursed again.

The saloon was almost empty, it being early in the evening. Clem ordered two beers. They took their drinks to a table in the corner.

Jeff ran through his suspicions. 'Well, at least we know now that Alexander Brown is trying to swindle us out of a piece of that land we bought fair and square.'

Clem was as puzzled as his brother. 'Why do you think Brown is so all-fired interested in it?'

Jeff shook his head. 'No idea.'

'Seems crazy,' said Clem. 'From what

Uncle Jim says, he's got more than enough range to the north of his spread if he wants to expand. That hunk of land is mostly scrub and shale, no good for cattle. After that it's foothills then mountains. Sure is a mystery why he wants it, even if he could persuade old man Schultz to sell a strip of his land so it could join up to his.'

Jeff rubbed his bristled chin. 'There's got to be a reason. Something we can't see at the moment.'

'Come on,' said Clem. 'Drink up. We've a long dark ride ahead of us.'

'And tomorrow, we got other work we promised to do,' Jeff shrugged.

10

The fire crackled away merrily in the pine-scented night air. Jeff threw on a couple of sticks and watched the smoke curl towards the star-filled sky. Away from the fire the night air had turned chill. He poured a cup of coffee, the hot liquid spreading a pleasing warmth through the whole of his body.

Temporarily he had put all thoughts of revenge on the land agent out of his mind. He had promised Uncle Jim that he would collect up a bunch of strays from the foothills, and now he sat content in the knowledge that he had fulfilled that promise.

Suddenly Jeff noticed Atlas's head come up, ears pricked. For some seconds he waited and watched, not moving a muscle, his eyes searching the shadows for some movement. Firelight reflected from Atlas's flank, the horse stamped its feet. Might be a bear or a cougar, Jeff thought. A long way off, a coyote howled at the moon.

A twig snapped somewhere in the gloom, the magnified sound like an explosion in the still night air. Instinctively Jeff pulled his revolver from its greased holster; the gun came out easily in his well-practised action.

'Hello, the camp,' a deep voice called from the darkness. 'Coffee smells good, mind if I sample some?'

'Come ahead,' Jeff replied, moving out of the brightness of the firelight.

The sound of leather-soled boots crunching over pine needles was accompanied by the much heavier thud of a horse's hoofs. Jeff stayed alert, his index finger resting easy on the trigger of his .44 calibre Remington New Model Army pistol.

Slowly, a shadowy figure emerged from the gloom, his sunburned features becoming clearer as the man moved further into the glow of the firelight. He was a big man, tall and broad, wearing a buff-coloured slicker, leading a tall bay. Jeff's own horses whinnied softly; the stranger's horse answered with a snort.

'Much obliged to you. Name's Michael French. Folks call me Mike.'

Jeff's grip on his revolver didn't relax. 'Jeff Jackson,' he called in response. 'Help yourself to some coffee.'

The stranger wrapped the horse's reins around a branch, and knelt on one knee. He moved slowly and deliberately, causing Jeff to remain cautious. The man poured a cup of coffee from the pot resting on a rock at the edge of the fire, tasted it then squatted on the ground. The slicker fell open, allowing Jeff to catch sight of the deep blue of an army blouse. The man pushed the slicker off his legs to reveal the lighter-blue colour of his breeches with a broad and stained yellow stripe down the side seam. Jeff noticed the stranger's boots — dusty, but they looked almost brand new.

'Army?' asked Jeff.

'Was,' answered the stranger. 'Union.'

'War's over, so why you still wearing the uniform?'

'Ain't got but these clothes, so I'm obliged to wear 'em.' The stranger took a long swallow from the tin cup. 'That coffee sure did taste good.'

Something in the stranger's manner began to put Jeff at ease. He holstered his pistol. 'Sorry about that.' He gestured with a nod of his head. 'No offence.'

'None taken. Man's got a right to protect himself,' the stranger drawled. 'Mind if I take another cup?'

'Help yourself.' Jeff squatted on the opposite side of the fire. 'So tell me, where you from, and what brings you to this neck of the woods?'

Mike French pushed his cavalry hat to the back of his head, revealing a face that was handsome and young-looking. 'You're certainly one for a direct question, Mr Jackson, and that's a fact.' Jeff ignored the comment. 'Well now, let me see. Mine's a familiar story, I guess.

Family home burned out, small tenant farm in Virginia, my folks dead and buried. Got a letter while I was away fighting. The unfamiliarity part is that as a dyed-in-the-wool southerner, I chose to fight for the North. When the war ended I decided I couldn't go back — don't believe my welcome would have been anything but a hot one. 'Sides, there was nothin' to go back for. Best choice seemed to be to head west, Montana goldfields seemed to have the right ring to it; big nuggets lying on the ground everywhere, folks said. Anyway, there she is — that's where Mike French is headed.'

He took off his hat, the white band at the top of his forehead where his hat had been contrasting strongly with his tanned face. He ran his hand through a luxuriant head of black hair.

'Mind if I take off my slicker?' he said. 'It's getting a mite warm.' Without waiting for Jeff's answer he pulled off the long raincoat and folded it neatly. 'Well, sir, that's my story, what about you? Were you in the war?'

Jeff could see that the stranger's well-worn uniform blouse was battle-stained; the three yellow stripes of a sergeant on both arms were unmissable. Around his waist sat a black leather army holster. Tucked into his belt was a smaller revolver, probably a .38.

'Yes, I was in the war. Same side as you,' Jeff added. 'My brother and me, plus our cousin, were in a mounted infantry brigade, 17th Indiana. We're from Evansville, Indiana. Went home, but couldn't settle back into a normal life, so we up-stakes and headed for Montana. My uncle owns a small spread; this is his land. I'm out picking up a few strays for him. Heading back to the ranch at first light.'

'Which direction?'

'North.'

'Mind if I tag along?'

'No, I'd welcome the company.' Jeff gestured to the pan sitting on a couple of stones. 'Few beans left. Need heating up, but you're welcome to them.' He pushed the blackened skillet back onto the fire.

'Thanks. That's right neighbourly of you.'

Jeff frowned. 'Hope you won't mind me saying, but it might be advisable not to wear your uniform.'

'Huh?' Mike replied indignantly.

'Could be mistaken for a deserter.' Jeff cringed inwardly at the sound of the words.

'That a problem round here?'

Jeff shook his head. 'Best not to chance it, I'd say.'

'One problem,' Mike said. 'These are the only clothes I got.'

'I can let you have a clean shirt. Be pleased to offer it.'

'Be pleased to accept,' answered Mike with a smile, helping himself to a plate of beans.

'You looking for a job?' asked Jeff.

'Wouldn't say no to one.'

'Done any cowpunching?'

'Some. Before the war.'

'OK, then. I'll talk to my uncle, see what he says.'

'Much obliged.'

'No promises, though,' Jeff cautioned.

'I understand.'

Jeff brewed up more coffee, and the two men settled down to get to know each other better.

'What's your uncle like?' Mike enquired.

'How do you mean?'

'Well, is he stern, friendly, what?'

'Oh. Guess you'd call him friendly, but I wouldn't want to tangle with him.'

Mike nodded and smiled. 'Seen any trouble round-abouts?'

The abrupt question took Jeff by surprise. 'Trouble?' he repeated. 'What kind of trouble?'

Mike shrugged, the firelight glowing bright on his cheeks and forehead. He took a sip of coffee. 'Rustlers?' he said.

Jeff thought over his response, deciding it was an honest question. 'Uncle Jim's had a few beeves taken.

Not as many as others in the valley,' he qualified.

'What about the local law?'

Jeff set down his tin cup. 'Sheriff Todd? He's not too convincing when it comes down to it.'

'How come?'

'Some say he's bought and paid for by the owner of the biggest spread around here, fellow called Alexander Brown. There's been talk his hands have been altering brands. Stuff like that.'

'You saying he's behind the rustling?'

'Heck no. It's probably folks putting two and two together to make five. Brown has bought out a couple of farmers and one or two of the smaller ranchers.'

Mike poured another coffee. 'It's an age-old story,' he commented ruefully. 'Big dog wants what the little dog has. Heard it was like that down in Texas before the war. Didn't take much to spark off a range war.'

'I don't think we're anywhere near

that,' Jeff grinned.

'Don't take much,' Mike opined. He sipped his coffee.

Jeff shrugged. 'It's late. I need to get some sleep,' he said stoically. 'We'll talk in the morning.'

The stranger took Jeff's meaning. 'OK. Night.' He got up from the fire and walked over to his horse, took off the saddle and tethered the animal next to the big black. Returning to the fire he threw on a couple of logs and settled down on his blanket, his head propped up on his saddle, pondering what Jeff had told him.

'Sort yourself out some fresh duds.' Jim Jackson gestured to the contents of a deep drawer he'd fetched from his bedroom tallboy. 'Hopefully they'll fit OK.'

'Much obliged,' said Mike.

'No trouble. Can't have you bein' forced to wear yer uniform, proud as you might be of it.'

Mike shot a glance at Jeff then dug out a couple of work-shirts, plus a pair of denim work-pants. 'I'll try these,' he said, taking them to try on and reappearing ten minutes later wearing his new rig. 'Sleeves and legs a mite on the short side, but they'll suit fine.' Mike grinned, hitching up his gunbelt.

Jeff noticed that the gunbelt wasn't the army-style version Mike had on earlier; this one was more like his own, cut away and tied down.

'What about socks and underwear?' asked Jim.

'Got some in my saddle-bags. But thanks.'

'OK,' chortled Jim, 'let's go eat.'

Over the course of the next few days Mike French settled into life as one of Jim Jackson's cowboys, showing his skill with horses and cattle.

'That's a nice young feller you found,' Jim confided to Jeff. 'He's a good worker. I like him a lot.'

Jeff smiled and slapped his uncle on the shoulder.

★   ★   ★

Billy Welch straddled a straight-backed chair.

'How's that foal doin'?' Clem asked.

A wholesome grin spread across Billy's boyish features. 'She's doin' right fine. Leg looks a treat.'

'Say, Billy,' Dan called out. 'You trying to grow a moustache?'

Billy's smiling expression turned sour, his hackles rising. 'What if I am?'

'Don't get riled,' Dan told him.

'You're always riling me.'

'No I ain't.'

'You are too.'

'Well. Your skin's as smooth as a baby's bottom.'

'Ain't.'

''Tis so. Only fluff on it.'

'Then how come you noticed my moustache, smart ass?'

Jeff and Clem laughed out loud at the banter.

'Where's Mike?' Billy enquired, changing the subject whilst turning his chair to face the breakfast table. No one answered, but Dan smirked at Clem, desperately fighting back a chuckle.

Cheng Li placed a mug of steaming coffee in front of the boy. 'Coffee, good,' he informed the new arrival, as if by some magic it would taste different this morning. Cheng Li gestured to a plate of piled-up food. 'Bacon, eggs,' he said, 'an your favelit — pahcakes!' The Chinaman beamed, wishing he could master the pronunciation of the English words. Cheng Li liked Billy, and had taken the young man under his wing.

Billy filled his plate to the intense pleasure of Cheng Li, and set about demolishing his breakfast.

Between forkfuls he repeated his earlier question: 'Where's Mike?'

Dan almost choked as Clem let out a guffaw.

Billy looked at the other diners. 'What?'

The Chinaman came to Billy's assistance before anyone could attempt an answer.

'Mike up eary. He go out.' Cheng Li

pointed somewhere west.

Billy filled his mouth like it would burst. 'I need to go look in on that foal,' he spluttered, his chair scraping across the wooden floorboards.

Everyone there knew what that meant.

'Don't forget you got chores,' Jeff called out.

'I won't,' yelled Billy as he reached the door.

'Better not!' shouted Jeff. The ranch house door banged shut.

Clem forked a piece of bacon into his mouth. 'That kid . . . ' He smiled as he let his words tail away. Dan grinned at his cousin, understanding the meaning of the unspoken words.

'Seems like every young man needs a hero to worship. I'd say Billy's found his,' Jeff said with a smile.

'You can say that again, cousin,' said Dan. 'He's bin doggin' Mike's footsteps ever since he met him.'

Out on the front porch, Billy sucked in a good lungful of crisp morning air, hitched up his belt and headed for the corral.

The pinto foal was pawing at the hard red earth. The herb-filled bandage Billy had applied to the foal's front right leg, although soiled, had done its job. A week ago the foal could hardly put its injured hoof to the ground.

The animal wandered over to the fence, allowing Billy to stroke his long black and white mane. Billy held out an apple, snaffled from Cheng Li's fruit bowl, on his palm. The animal gobbled it up then snorted and snuffled Billy's outstretched hand.

'You'll soon be strong enough to run like the wind,' he told the horse, digging deep into the pocket of his jeans. He came up with a walnut. The horse, scenting the delicacy, pushed Billy's closed hand with his nose until the young man opened his fingers. The foal's eyes twinkled. A split second later the shell of the nut cracked open under the pressure of the foal's strong teeth. Billy pulled out another and fed it to the contented animal.

'No more.' He patted the horse and headed away from the corral, ignoring the pinto's whinnying for him to come back with more walnuts.

Billy decided to walk down to the river where a couple of walnut trees would allow him to replenish his stock. He whistled a tune as he wandered jauntily across the lush pastureland; not a care in the world.

His thoughts turned to his ma and pa, and his four older siblings back home in Indiana. His mother hadn't wanted him to leave home; tears flowing down her cheeks she had pleaded with him not to go. His father had understood, and had supported Billy's wanderlust. Billy brushed away the melancholy notions, and began to whistle again.

As he neared the crest of a small hillock, he heard the sharp retort of a pistol, the harsh sound drifting on the gentle wind. Billy pulled up sharp. Another shot rang out followed by two more in fast succession.

Billy's youthful curiosity drew him to the sound like a magnet. He moved forward cautiously, removing his hat as he breasted the small ridge overlooking the river. He peered through the foliage of the trees, seeing the instigator of the gunshots.

Mike French was adjusting a target tacked to the broad trunk of a tree. Billy watched Mike check his six-gun, spin the chamber twice then slide the weapon into the holster that was tied down on his thigh with a thin strand of smooth rawhide. Unhurriedly Mike picked up a couple of small stones from the grassy bank above the gurgling river. One after the other he tossed the pebbles into the air, volleying each one into the water with his right foot. Seemingly satisfied with his dexterity, Mike hitched up the gunbelt then turned away from the target, walking briskly with deliberate steps. Billy counted silently under his breath. On the twelfth step Mike swivelled, spinning in a blur of a single movement as the Colt that had suddenly appeared in his right hand barked out twice.

Billy had never seen anything like it; he had never believed anyone could draw and shoot that fast. He was mesmerized and in awe as Mike holstered his gun and ambled to the tree to check the target. Tipping back his Stetson, Mike took out the Colt and reloaded. That was Billy's signal to show himself.

He called out a greeting, his young voice clear above the sounds of the river. Mike looked up, and — recognizing who had shouted — raised a hand in acknowledgement.

Billy couldn't wait to get down the slope, finding it difficult to hide his admiration and at one point almost slipping and losing his balance, threatening to fall headlong into Mike's path.

'Mike!' he grinned. 'That sure was some shooting.'

Mike smiled and holstered his Colt. 'Morning, Billy, you're out early.'

Billy dragged his gaze from his hero, and took a look at the target. There were eight bullet holes grouped around the centre of a three-inch circle. 'How many shots you take?' he asked.

'Eight,' answered Mike.

Billy's hero worship went into overdrive. 'Where'd you learn to shoot like that?' Billy's expression was one of earnest enthusiasm.

Mike grinned, recognizing how he had felt years earlier when as a youth he'd asked a similar question. 'Practice. And more practice,' he said.

Billy was dying to ask another question; he finally got up sufficient courage to ask it. 'Will you teach me how to shoot like that?' His eyes were like those of an expectant puppy.

Mike's face took on a more serious expression. 'Why would you want to learn that?'

'I'd just love to be able to draw and shoot that fast.'

'Why?' Mike asked sympathetically. 'Guns are dangerous.'

'Not if you can draw that fast.'

'You're wrong there, Billy. Quite the opposite is true.'

'No way.'

'There's always someone faster, Billy.'

'Nobody's faster than you, Mike. Nobody.'

Mike placed an arm around Billy's shoulders. 'Being fast with a gun can be a curse.' Mike could see Billy was puzzled by his caution. 'Once you get a reputation as a gunslinger, no matter how small, it acts like a magnet, drawing other gunmen who think they are faster than you. A gunfight is nigh on impossible to avoid when you've got a man in your face calling you a coward. You can't back down, so you have to kill him, or else he'll kill you.' Mike's eyes were sad. 'Killing a man ain't something to aspire to, Billy. And remember, each time you survive a duel, your reputation swells and the number of men who want to take your scalp increases. It's a vicious circle you do not want to get on. Trust me, there are much more important things in life to aspire to.'

Mike wasn't sure that Billy understood his advice. He felt the need to say more. 'So, no, Billy. I won't teach you how to kill people.' He gave Billy's shoulder a squeeze. 'Come on. Let's get back, we got work to do.'

Billy trudged along miserably in the wake of his hero, hugely disappointed, but not defeated. He'd practise on his own. He would show them.

All through supper Billy's hangdog expression was clear as day. Mike had told Jeff and the others what had happened and all agreed he had done the right thing. They decided it was best to ignore Billy's misery and hope he would soon get over his disappointment.

Clem turned to Jeff. 'Come on. It's our turn on the range tonight. We got cows to nursemaid.'

★ ★ ★

Jeff tugged the blanket round his legs against the chill night air, considering the positive fact that the week had been productive. The herd of wild horses had almost doubled; they'd soon have enough for the first shipment to Fort Ellis. However, there was still the negative problem of the disputed land — that still had to be resolved.

He was careful not to show it, but the dispute was eating away at his insides. It wasn't so much that the lawsuit might be lost, it was the fact that they had been cheated on his watch; he didn't care for that notion one iota. For a while he lay quietly wondering what he should have done differently. He closed his tired eyes; a welcome, peaceful sleep descended upon him.

It was still dark when Clem nudged Jeff's shoulder. 'Your watch,' he said.

11

'No. You two go. It's me and Billy's turn to help Uncle Jim,' Dan offered.

'You sure?' asked Clem.

'Just make sure you get that big white,' Dan ordered.

On the previous evening Dan and Clem had spotted a small herd of wild ponies near the small falls on the Boulder River.

'You're sure?'

'Certain,' replied Dan. 'Get going. And don't forget what I said.' Dan waved as he and Billy spurred away. Clem and Jeff headed west.

Two hours of hard riding and they were splashing their mounts into the ford across the Boulder River, letting their horses take a drink.

Clem leaned on the pommel of his saddle. 'They were heading thataway' — he pointed west through the heat haze — 'towards that ravine.'

'How many?' asked Jeff.

'About twenty, maybe more.' Clem kicked his mount forward into an easy trot.

The land rose steadily as they left the river behind. On the crest of a grassy knoll Clem abruptly reined in his horse. 'Look.' He pointed. 'Three riders?'

Jeff tugged his telescope from his saddle-bag. 'Can't really see who they are. But, the middle rider is a much larger man than the other two.'

'Let me see.' Clem held out a gloved hand. He steadied the telescope and let out a low whistle. 'That big guy looks like Alexander Brown.'

'Well,' Jeff grimaced, 'whoever they are they're crossing our land.'

'Let's go see,' suggested Clem as the riders disappeared into a stand of firs on the edge of the foothills.

The rough trail was intersected by a number of other less discernible paths. Despite the absence of hoof-prints the brothers stayed on the most obvious, winding in and out of trees and around rocky outcrops — hard going for horse and man alike. The wild countryside was beautiful, but getting colder by the minute. High above, snow-capped peaks seemed to fill the cloudless sky, the air heavy with the scent of pine and cedar. A snow-cold wind gusted between the trees. Jeff pulled the collar of his coat higher.

After almost one hour of climbing, the narrow path curled around the edge of a fifty-foot-high wall of rock. To the right the ground fell away to a sheer drop.

Jeff cursed under his breath. He turned in the saddle, saddle leather creaking as he changed his weight. 'Trail's vanished!'

Clem peered beyond his brother, dismayed by the sight that greeted his eyes.

'I don't understand it.' The frustration in Jeff's voice was clear.

'Let's backtrack and find a way around this,' suggested Clem, backing his horse to a small clearing. Jeff followed suit.

Shale and stones crunched and slipped under their horses' hoofs to clatter away down the steep slope; the going grew tougher. More than once they were forced to seek out an alternative route. It was as though this mountain was reluctant to give up its secrets; hopefully the men they were trailing were finding the going equally arduous.

The sound of water, loud as a strong wind, filled the air as they rode out of a stand of cedars. The faintest thread of a game trail skirted a rushing stream.

The horses splashed noisily through a side-pool, animals and riders spattered by spray. The trail turned ninety degrees right then sharp left. Atlas shied at the sight ahead. A dark, narrow cleft ran between two overhanging rock faces; it would be a tight squeeze.

Jeff touched his spurs, urging the big horse forward. Atlas snorted a protest, but walked on.

On either side, the sheer rock appeared to press inwards, making passage appear tighter than it was. Overhead, the rocks towered to over thirty feet, boulders and vegetation closing in places like the inside of a cave. For more than ten minutes the brothers walked their horses in deep shadow before entering a coppice of firs.

At the edge of a clearing another gushing stream cascaded down an overhanging rock face before falling away to a deep chasm. Mist and spray rose to obscure the opposite side of the ravine.

Once past the shelter of the overhanging cliff they came upon an area of flat, lush grass.

'Horses could do with a rest,' Clem observed.

Jeff nodded and reined in Atlas. The brothers dismounted and loose-tethered their mounts.

'Think we lost 'em?' Jeff said drily.

'Looks that way,' Clem agreed.

The silence was almost deafening. Not even the mewing of a bird of prey wheeling high in the sky broke the stillness; it was as if the world had gone to sleep.

Then out of the blue came the distant but unmistakable whinny of a horse.

Both heads turned to face the sound, searching to confirm what they had heard.

Clem looked at the horses, concerned that one of them might give an answering whinny; but both animals were happily cropping grass.

Another sound came a few minutes later; a mini rock slide, the kind made when a horse steps on loose stones. In one movement Jeff had the telescope out of his saddle-bag and up to his eye, focusing on the opposite side of the ravine. For a moment nothing came into view except leaves and the trunks of trees, then the faintest glimpse between two trees, something that clearly was not part of the natural landscape. A sorrel horse with a white forehead being ridden by the prospector they'd seen in Gallatin City. Jeff realized his mistake in electing to take the more obvious of the two trails. The spot he was looking at was on the opposite side of the ravine, fifteen to twenty feet higher.

Jeff kept the telescope focused on the gap in the trees; the sight of a familiar second rider swam into view. Jeff passed the telescope swiftly to Clem, who focused on the spot he indicated. The large bulk of Alexander Brown bobbed into vision, his horse blowing visibly, struggling with the demands of the steep slope and the weight of its rider.

'That who I think it is?' whispered Jeff.

'Alexander Brown for certain,' Clem replied in a hushed tone. 'Wait.' Clem's mouth dried unexpectedly with excitement. 'The third rider is that gunhand, calls himself the Lafayette Kid.'

'Where d'you suppose they're going?' Jeff asked. 'And more to the point

— why?' His voice changed to a whisper. 'Mount up.'

Twenty or more minutes of steep climbing brought them to a second small clearing.

Something like a shout drifted across the ravine, halting Jeff in his tracks.

'Hear that?' he whispered.

Clem hadn't heard anything other than the gentle wind in the trees. 'What was it?' he asked.

Just then the breeze shifted direction, and the rhythmic smack of steel on rock echoed across the ravine. Jeff slipped from his saddle, grabbing his rifle. Clem dismounted slowly and slid his rifle from its saddle holster. Looping the reins of their lathered horses around the branch of a juniper bush, they began to scale the sloping rock in the direction of the sound, the rough surface making the climb relatively easy.

Backs bent low, the brothers tiptoed to the summit. They dropped down onto their bellies after removing their hats, inching forward to the edge. The south side of the deep ravine they'd climbed had closed up, the northern side now just a stone's throw away. The rock on which they lay was high above a wide clearing. There, below, in plain sight were the three men they had tracked.

The prospector was hard at work swinging a long-handled pickaxe. He was hammering at a cleft in the rock, sweating profusely. Alexander Brown was watching the toiling man intently. The Lafayette Kid lounged on a flat rock, seemingly uninterested in the noisy goings-on not twenty feet from him. A cigarette dangled from his thin lips, eyes squinting against the smoke that curled upwards. In his right hand he held a six-gun; he was spinning the cylinder repetitively across the palm of his other hand.

The Kid looked up as a small section of rock, dislodged by the prospector's pickaxe, tumbled to the ground with a dull thud, splitting into many parts. The prospector went down onto one knee, searching through the smaller pieces of rock.

A harsh grunt preceded the discarding of several shards before finally a wide grin spread across his weather-beaten face. He stood, toting a rock which he held out towards Brown. 'See this?' he said excitedly. 'S'what we came fer.'

Brown took the rock and examined it. 'Silver. By God!' he yelled, tracing a gloved finger over the uneven surface.

The words drifted clearly up to where the brothers lay. Clem silently mouthed one word at his brother: 'Silver!'

Jeff scanned the clearing through the telescope; the place had a cold aura, now he saw why.

Short totem poles carved with grotesque faces stared at the intruders. Wreaths of long feathers hung motionless from boughs of trees. Decorated shields and lances hung from poles, and at the far end of the clearing stood two raised burial pyres, ghostly grey in contrast to the greens and browns of the foliage. There was no mistaking what this place was, silent until the stillness had been shattered by the ringing peal of steel upon rock.

The prospector paused to wipe a sleeve across his forehead. He spat on the ground.

'Like I told ya,' he grinned toothlessly, turning to face Brown. 'It's a mother lode. Top quality. Richest ore I ever see'd.'

The Kid came alert.

Alexander Brown clapped the prospector on the back. 'Good man,' he praised. 'What do you reckon?'

The prospector squinted and closed one eye while he computed, his face a picture of concentration. 'Four, maybe five men should do it. We can rig up a chute and slide the ore down the valley where we can work it.'

'Agreed,' chirped Brown.

The prospector looked up. 'Fifty-fifty? Like we said?'

Brown shot a glance at the Kid, who

got up and ambled over.

'No! Not fifty-fifty,' Brown answered harshly.

The prospector stiffened, his sun-burned features tightened, his voice became agitated. 'You said, if'n I showed you where the silver was we'd be partners. That's fifty-fifty.'

Brown shook his head. 'I have new partners.' Brown's voice was even, emotionless, but steel-like. 'Remember, this is my land, so you'll be working for me. I will provide the protection and the necessary finance. You will work the seam. You'll find me more than generous.'

The prospector looked like he was about to burst. 'Why you dirty, low-down backslider.'

'Watch your mouth,' snapped Brown.

'You think you can rob me? Push me around? I found this strike. Not you. Me! So by rights it's mine — '

'Wrong!' interrupted Brown. 'My land! My silver!' he shouted, turning away. 'Let's get back to town,' he said.

The prospector's anger exploded. He grabbed the discarded pickaxe and swung it upwards.

A single shot rang out before the tool reached the top of its arc. The pick clattered to the ground as the prospector jerked before being propelled backward a couple of steps by the force of the big .45 calibre bullet that tore into his chest.

The Lafayette Kid blew the smoke from the muzzle of his Colt before holstering the weapon, a sickly wickedness written across his face.

For a second, Alexander Brown watched the blood pump from the prospector's chest, the stench of burnt gunpowder in his nostrils. Then he spat out the acrid taste from his mouth. He turned, staring at the Kid with fury in his eyes.

'Saved yer bacon there, boss,' the Kid sneered.

'We needed him,' Brown stormed.

'I'll find somebody else. Leave it to me.' The Kid's voice was matter-of-fact, unfazed by the anger in his employer's eyes.

Brown looked questioningly at the Kid, wondering exactly what kind of Pandora's Box he had opened by employing such a killer. His mouth dried.

The Kid broke the silence. 'You'll be in business in less than a week,' he told him.

Brown recovered his voice, and his composure. 'No!' he corrected, his anger subsiding. 'Not until the question of my clear title to this land has been finalized.' He clenched his huge fists. 'You heard McCall. Two weeks, he said. Two weeks!' Brown pointed to the ground. 'Fill the saddle-bags with those rocks. We'll get the ore analyzed.'

'What about him?' The Kid pointed at the prone body.

'Buzzards will make short work of him.'

The Kid bent over the body, emptied the pockets, taking anything of value before tearing away the prospector's clothing. 'Give 'em a head start,' he sneered, looking down at the naked body.

The Kid stuffed the remnants of the prospector's clothes into a gunny sack tied to the prospector's sorrel, then collected the ore and stowed it safely inside his and Brown's saddle-bags.

Killer and employer mounted and wheeled away. Brown led the way out of the clearing: two men, three horses — one man less than went up the mountain.

Certain that Brown and his henchman were out of earshot, Jeff turned to his brother. 'So now we know.'

'Silver,' said Clem, 'seems to have the power to make men do the worst things.'

The two brothers climbed down into the clearing.

Jeff kicked a lump of ore. 'Help me move the body over by those burial pyres. We'll cover it with stones to keep varmints from eating the evidence.'

Clem was puzzled. 'What? Leave the body here?'

'For now. We'd never get it over to where our horses are tethered, and there's no way to get the horses over to this side. So this poor feller is going to have to stay here until we can come back up the other trail. Gather up a few bits of ore; we'll take it to the assay office and have it valued ourselves.'

'Good thinking,' said Clem. 'Should we tell Sheriff Todd about this?'

'No point. Remember he's Brown's man, bought and paid.'

'There's always the law in Gallatin City,' said Clem.

'Yep! Probably our best option. But when we get back we'll go see Nagel and tell him what we've seen. Write out what we witnessed, and sign it as our sworn affidavit. Then I say we should tell Ika what's happened and where. I'll bet her people will want to know what Alexander Brown's been up to on their sacred burial grounds.' Jeff thought about what he had said. 'Only trouble is . . . '

'What?'

'Whatever we do or say, it'll be our word against Brown's, and he can pay for enough witnesses of his own to say whatever he wants them to. Heck, he might even accuse us of the killing.'

'Christ alive!' exclaimed Clem. 'You really think he would?'

'Wouldn't put it past him.'

12

Alexander Brown's muttered obscenities knew no limit. He'd known the Kid's reputation as a wild, cold-blooded killer; that's why he had hired him in the first place. Only now did Brown recognize the naïvety in expecting such a man to curb his natural instinct to kill.

He had purchased the threat of force such men brought to the table and had harnessed that force to pressurize people to bend to his will. However, witnessing at first hand the cold-blooded killing of the prospector had both shocked and surprised him; it had never been part of the plan. Disarming the old man would have been easy, and mighty preferable. Brown figured he could have worked everything out with the old-timer. The Kid didn't need to kill the old galoot. He could have shouted out a warning. That would have been sufficient for Brown to sidestep the pickaxe.

Brown swallowed another whiskey to dull any more negative thoughts and pondered the riches opening up to him — his fierce ambition would surely see him through.

So what that the man had died — he didn't know him, had only met him three times. And in any case, it had been his own fault that he had died; he was the first to adopt a violent approach — stupid fool.

Hopefully the wild beasts on the mountain would soon obliterate all evidence of wrongdoing. Red had already re-branded the prospector's horse and put it in the remuda. The Kid had promised to burn the prospector's clothes; after that there were no loose ends that needed tying up. And in any case, so what if the law got involved? He owned the law; Sheriff Todd would ride to orders, he wouldn't do anything without being told what to do.

What's to worry about? Brown asked himself. Nothing at all, was the answer. Everything was still going to plan.

After supper Alexander Brown sat at his huge oak desk rethinking his plans for the future. The log fire burned nicely, warming the room to a pleasant temperature. He poured three fingers of Tennessee's finest. Sipping the bourbon, he leaned back into the deep leather padding of the chair, stretching his legs to relieve the stiffness of the long hard ride. From the humidor on his desk he took a long thin cigar, gently squeezing the tube of tightly rolled tobacco, a faint smile of anticipation on his lips.

Swivelling to face the fire, he leaned forward to light a long spiller which he touched to the end of the cigar. Leaning back in the chair he drew the smoke into his mouth, holding it there to appreciate the flavour, allowing the smoke to linger. Another sip of bourbon enhanced his appreciation of the moment.

Soon, not only would he be the biggest rancher in the territory, but probably the richest. A man with the kind of wealth he would soon have would find it easy to buy the governorship.

Perhaps he would marry again, he pondered, sad that his wife had died in childbirth fifteen years earlier and that he was childless following the death of his son. At forty-nine years old he was still young enough to start a family.

He sucked in another mouthful of tobacco smoke and mentally ran through a list of women who might fit the bill as the future Mrs Alexander Brown; there weren't many, he had to admit. Maybe he'd take a trip back east, see what he could find. Although, there was one suitable candidate closer to hand. Lars Andersen's daughter, Laurie. Now, there was a handsome woman, as good-looking a female as he had ever seen. What would she be? Twenty? Twenty-one? Couldn't be much more. Great figure, lovely hair, and nice to talk to from what he recalled. Yes! The more he thought about her, the surer he became. Laurie Andersen would do very nicely.

Long before the cigar was finished Alexander Brown was fully relaxed and contented. He retired to bed feeling rather pleased with himself.

★ ★ ★

After a hearty breakfast of steak and eggs Alexander Brown called for his favourite horse to be saddled. He ordered his foreman and two of his cowhands plus the Lafayette Kid to accompany him on a trip to Gallatin City — his third in two weeks.

Before leaving, Brown called the Kid over. 'Did you see to that problem in White Bluff?'

'All sorted,' the kid grinned. 'Gettin' him to draw was easy.'

'What about his pa?'

'Let's just say they've been reunited in heaven.'

Brown gave the Kid a grateful pat on the shoulder, finding the power to control life and death a powerful drug.

The polished brass plaque on the wall of the smart, red-brick building proclaimed that the first-floor suite of offices were occupied by Stewart McCall, Attorney At Law; a string of qualifications followed.

Sunlight streamed through the large, dual-aspect windows lighting the warm room, illuminating the elegant furnishings of the lawyer's office.

Seeing who had entered, immaculately dressed Lawyer McCall rose from behind the wide red leather-topped desk; an embarrassed clerk fussed behind the unannounced and unexpected Alexander Brown.

'Stewart.' Brown held out a large hand.

The lawyer shook Brown's hand warmly. 'Alexander. How nice to see you.' A strong whiff of freshly sprayed cologne hung pungent in the air. The clerk closed the door behind the visitors.

Lawyer McCall eyed the two men behind his richest client. Red West, he knew, the other he had only seen once before, and from the mad-dog look in the thin man's eyes he would have preferred to avoid seeing him today; he had the look of a volcano about him.

Brown saw the lawyer's quizzical expression. 'Don't mind them,' he said smoothly. 'They're witnesses.'

'Fine. Welcome, gentlemen,' McCall said. 'Please take a seat.'

Red West and the Kid elected to sit against the wallpapered walls on either side of the door.

McCall turned his focus back to Alexander Brown. 'Alexander.' The lawyer indicated a plush chaise longue for his client to rest his rich hide upon. Since becoming Alexander Brown's legal representative Stewart McCall's fortune had risen steadily. 'Cognac?' he asked. Brown nodded.

From an antique decanter McCall poured out two good measures into crystal tumblers. Both men took a sip.

'Your men?' asked the lawyer.

'They don't drink on duty,' replied Brown.

The Kid and Red West exchanged disappointed glances. The Kid shrugged and took out the makings. He commenced to roll a cigarette.

Before he had finished fashioning his slender creation McCall said, 'I would prefer it if you wouldn't smoke in my office.'

The Kid pretended he hadn't heard and lit up. He blew a smoke ring of defiance in the direction of the lawyer. McCall looked at Brown for support.

'Let's get down to business,' snapped the big Scotsman.

McCall returned to his seat behind the desk; he knew when he was being told to leave it. He allowed a smile to form on his thin lips. He spread his hands, palms upwards, and gave a polite nod. 'Indeed,' he said.

'Are the documents ready?' Brown demanded, his voice gruff and loud.

'Yes, Alexander.'

'You're certain they'll hold up under examination?' he growled.

'Absolutely,' McCall gushed. 'Everything is as tight as a drum.' He wrung his oily hands.

McCall swung round in his seat to face a large safe, spinning the tumbler back and forth, making sure to hide the combination from prying eyes. The safe door opened smoothly. McCall reached inside and took out two black leather-bound folders and two rolled-up maps. Moving all obstacles out of the way, he spread the contents on the desk.

Brown examined the documents minutely. 'These signatures,' Brown pointed, 'you're sure about these?'

'First things first.' McCall bit his lip. 'Sorry. I mean, shall we get the Schultz ranch out of the way first?'

Brown nodded.

'Here are the deeds and the bill of sale. You sign under where Schultz signed,' McCall chortled. 'He didn't, of course.'

McCall's attempted humour was lost

on Brown; he signed.

'Now the two witnesses.' West and the Kid signed where McCall indicated.

'Where is the cash?' McCall enquired.

'Banker's cheque,' Brown corrected. He looked questioningly at the Kid.

'In Schultz's coat pocket,' the Kid answered.

'Good,' McCall greased. 'You are now the legitimate owner of the Bar S ranch. Shall we move on to the Jackson land?'

'Answer my question about the signatures,' Brown ordered.

McCall smiled greasily. 'Best forgeries you will ever see. Trust me.'

'I am trusting you,' Brown said brusquely, 'and you'd better not breach that trust.'

McCall flinched, his thin smile turning sour at Brown's word of warning.

'Let's see the map,' Brown barked.

Lawyer McCall obeyed, weighting down the corners of the heavy parchment. Brown's eyes took in every detail.

Satisfied, Brown grunted, pointing at

another of the documents. 'This where you want me and the boys to sign?'

McCall nodded. Brown took the pen he was offered and signed where the lawyer indicated; West and the Kid signed as requested. McCall pressed a half-moon blotter to the fresh ink then appended his own signature and a date.

'Voilà!' he exclaimed.

Brown looked at the date — three months earlier. He took out a snakeskin wallet, extracted a twenty dollar bill. 'Red, you and the Kid go get yourselves a drink and a little female entertainment, you've earned it.'

The Kid's face was absent of emotion. Red grinned and slipped the money into his pocket; he made no move to leave.

Brown laughed out loud. 'I haven't forgotten, Red.'

Lawyer McCall handed Brown two bulging envelopes.

'One for you' — Brown pressed one envelope into Red's open hand — 'and one for you,' he added, handing the other envelope to the Kid. Both recipients grinned broadly. 'I'll see you at the hotel later.'

The two gunmen trooped out slowly, closing the door behind them.

Brown turned back to his lawyer. He took another sip of brandy; the liquid somehow tasted even smoother this time. 'You're certain all this is water-tight?'

'Absolutely! Absolutely!' McCall repeated. He was about to add, 'trust me,' but thought the better of it.

'I've heard the Jacksons have hired Nagel to represent them.'

'Yes. But we need have no worries, Alexander. We always knew they would challenge your title to the land. Didn't we? But there's nothing to worry about, they don't have a leg to stand on.' He raised his glass, about to offer up a toast.

Brown butted in. 'Where are the originals?' he snarled.

'Where no one will ever find them,' the lawyer replied nervously.

'And where's that?'

'Destroyed, Alexander, destroyed,' he lied. The originals were safely under lock and key, an insurance should there be a problem in the future. McCall smiled inwardly at his own cleverness.

Brown grunted. 'What about the land agent?'

McCall shook his head. 'He's been paid plenty to keep his mouth shut. He won't talk.'

Brown grunted again. 'Why destroy the originals?' McCall quickly put his trembling hands under the desk. 'Might we not need them one day?'

The lawyer rushed his answer. 'No!' He clenched his fists to alleviate the growing tension suddenly sweeping away his confidence. 'There is no reason why we would ever need them.' He was calmer now. 'Not even to guard against either party not keeping to their side of the bargain.' As soon as the words left his lips he knew he'd said the wrong thing.

Brown's dark eyes smouldered indignantly. 'What's that supposed to mean?'

McCall felt his armpits flood with sweat; no suitable words came into his head. Eventually under the pressure of Brown's fixed stare he muttered out one word. 'Nothing.'

Brown decided to let it go, for the moment at any rate. He'd already decided that in the not too distant future he would need a new legal representative because his present one would be dead, along with the land agent.

'What will we do when the Jacksons make their challenge?' asked Brown.

McCall was happy to have extracted himself from what looked for a moment like a tricky situation. 'By then, Alexander, they will already be in custody.'

'On what charge?'

'Attempted falsification of deeds, and trespass,' McCall answered smugly. 'They will produce their copy of the, er . . . *alleged*' — he smiled at his use of the word — 'transaction. We will produce our documents which pre-date theirs. The land agent will testify in our favour and the judge will rule against their claim.' Elbows on the desk, McCall steepled his hands together, as if intending to kiss his fingertips. 'Nothing is more certain.' He suppressed a chortle of smugness. 'The Jackson boys will be found guilty of perjury as well as falsification of official documents. They are certain to be jailed,' he added with a chuckle.

Brown looked questioningly at his lawyer. 'How can you be so sure of all this?'

'Let us just say that I have an intimate understanding with Judge Grimes.'

'Good man.' Brown rose and headed for the door. McCall rushed around the desk and across the room to get to the door handle first. He held out a hand, Brown took it. 'I know you won't let me down,' Brown said firmly.

McCall recognized the veiled threat.

He turned the brass handle and opened the door.

Brown turned on his heel and left the lawyer feeling like a child who'd got caught with his hand in the cookie jar.

13

The thunder of hoofs stopped abruptly as Sanchez reined in his sweat-plastered horse.

'Boss! Boss!' he shouted.

Jim Jackson emerged from the barn. 'What's up?

'Wire, boss. Along Pitcher's Creek.' Sanchez was out of breath.

'Where?'

'Where the creek turns north to meet the Boulder River, near Schultz's boundary.' Sanchez gulped in air.

'What?' Jim got Sanchez to tell him again everything he knew. 'Sanchez. Ride out to Jeff's place. Tell him and the boys to meet me at Schultz's ranch. Cut out a fresh horse.' Jim turned. 'Mike, you come with me an' the rest of the boys.'

Nervous horses snorted anxiously as Jim Jackson banged on the door of

Schultz's small ranch house, Mike French at his side. The door creaked open. Instinctively Jim's and Mike's hands swept down to their six-guns as they took a step inside.

'Schultz!' Jim called out. 'Walter!'

Outside, twenty minutes later, Jeff, Clem, Dan and Billy reined in their horses and leaped to the ground; Sanchez followed. Jim and Mike appeared in the doorway.

Clem greeted his uncle with a question. 'Where is everybody?'

Jim Jackson looked at the newcomers, sadness written all over his face. 'Place is deserted.'

'What about the barn and outbuildings?' asked Jeff.

'Nothin'!'

'How many riders did Schultz have working for him?'

'Three or four, plus his son, Walt Junior.' Jim sat down on the step.

Sanchez appeared from the bunkhouse. 'Place is pretty much cleaned out, boss.'

'We've seen the wire,' said Jeff, 'somebody wants to keep your cows from that water.'

'Bastards!' cursed Jim. 'I hate wire.'

'You figure it was Brown's boys, boss?'

'More'n likely. Wouldn't have been Walter, that's fer sure.' Jim thought for a moment. 'Jeff, will you go into White Bluff, see if you can find out where Walt and his son are? The rest of you come with me. Let's go tear that wire down.'

'I'll go with Jeff,' Mike pronounced.

* * *

'Schultz's son dead?' Jeff couldn't believe what he was hearing.

Doctor Hollis nodded solemnly.

'How'd he die?' asked Mike.

'Gunfight, day before yesterday. He was in the saloon. Kid came in. There was an argument. Both went for their guns. The Kid was fast. Young Schultz never had a chance. His six-gun never even cleared his holster.'

'The Kid?' Mike asked.

The doctor sighed. 'Fellow calls himself the Lafayette Kid.'

'The Lafayette Kid, well I'll be . . . '

Jeff was puzzled. 'Sounds like you know him, Mike.'

'Don't know him, but I've heard of him,' Mike corrected. 'What was the argument about?'

'Who knows? Women? Drink? The war? Who knows?' The doctor was obviously upset. 'There was nothing I could do, he was dead before I got there.'

'Where's his body?'

'Kurt carried him over to Dieter's.'

'What about his father? Does Walt know what's happened? Anybody seen him?'

Doctor Hollis scratched his beard. 'I sent a rider out to his ranch. Walt wasn't there, only one of his cowhands, Tom Gantley, and he was about to leave; seems that the rest had already lit out. Tom said he hadn't seen Walter for three or four days, said young Schultz had been out looking for his pa every day, but had found nothing. Last thing he knew was what Schultz's kid told him, that last Friday his pa had met Alexander Brown on the trail. The two men had argued fiercely about something. Then Schultz had told his son to go back to the ranch, he was going someplace with Brown.'

'That's a long time to be away from home without leaving word, don't you think?'

'Sure do, Jeff.'

'Has anyone asked Brown what he knows about Walt going missing?'

'Asked him myself, day before yesterday.'

'What'd he say?'

'Said he hadn't seen Walter since Friday. Confirmed they'd argued. Brown said it was about the price he was willing to pay for the Bar S.'

'Schultz was selling?'

'Not was. Did,' Hollis said. 'Brown told me he'd bought the Bar S and was waiting for word from Schultz that he had cleared the place. Offered to show me the bill of sale.'

'We've just been out to Schultz's ranch, the place is deserted. And there's wire been strung on our side of the river.'

'That wouldn't have been Schultz. I know how much he hated wire. You can bet your life that's Brown's doing.'

'You think something's happened to Schultz, Doc?' Mike asked.

'Can't think of another reason for him to go missing.'

'You think he might be dead?' asked Jeff.

Doctor Hollis scratched at his beard. 'I guess it kinda looks that way, Jeff.'

Mike sought clarification. 'You certain it was the Lafayette Kid who shot young Schultz?'

'Whitish hair. Dressed in black. Wearing a pair of back-to-front Colts. That's the Kid, ain't it?' Hollis said.

'Sure is,' Mike and Jeff chorused.

14

Boulder River Canyon

'That all of them?' Clem asked, reining in his horse.

'I reckon,' sighed Dan, watching the skittish mustangs mill around the corral. 'That big black's the lead stallion; he'll fetch top dollar. I've got a halter on him; the rest'll follow.' Dan was pleased with his work, and rightfully so; he'd saddle-broken the best six of the bunch to sell separately. 'Them six'll make fine officers' mounts,' he said.

'Billy still aiming to stay behind to look after that foal?'

'Yep. Says he's also gonna help Jim start the round-up. Jim reckons there's too many of them critters up on the high flats need fetching down before winter sets in. He wants to be sure there's none on Bar S land, now Brown owns it.'

'Sooner him than me,' Clem chuckled. 'I know which I'd rather be doing.
Should be able to have a good time
after we deliver the first batch of
mustangs to Fort Ellis. What do you
say?'

Dan returned Clem's enthusiastic
grin. 'I'm with you, cousin,' he said.
'Say, where's Jeff?'

'Should be here soon. Went into
White Bluff last night to see Laurie.'

'Getting a mite serious, ain't it?'

'Looks that way,' answered Clem.
'But who can blame him? She sure is
one fine-looking gal, and that's a fact.'
He pushed his hat away from his
forehead and wiped his brow. 'Mike
coming with us?'

'Said so.' Dan shielded his eyes from
the sun's glare. 'If I'm not mistaken
that's him now.'

Clem peered into the distance.
'That's him all right, I'd recognize that
big bay of his anywhere.'

Minutes later Mike French reined in
his horse. 'Clem, Dan,' he greeted. He

202

looked at the horses in the corral. 'Fine-lookin' bunch, ain't they?' His eyes rested on the big black with the halter. 'That one's a beaut.'

'Needs gelding,' Dan said, 'but he is magnificent, that's for sure.'

'We startin' out this afternoon or leavin' it till tomorrow?' Mike enquired.

'Soon as Jeff gets back we'll make a start. Should be here soon.'

'He in town?' Mike drawled.

Clem nodded. Dan and Mike smiled knowingly.

Twenty minutes later Jeff rode up. Half an hour later they hit the trail.

15

The Bar-B saloon, White Bluff

'Sheriff, something has to be done about them pesky Indians.' Ed Howes scratched his bushy beard.

'I'm only one man, Ed. There's very little I can do other than what I done already.'

'An' what's that?'

'I sent riders out to warn the settlers within thirty miles.' Ed tried to butt in, but the sheriff held up a hand to forestall the man's next question. 'And I've sent reports to the army at Fort Ellis.'

Heads turned as the saloon doors swung open.

'Just the man I want to see,' Ed Howes called out.

Jim Jackson ambled to the bar, Billy Welch in tow.

'What's up, Ed?' Jim asked.

'You heard about the Sioux raids on the small ranches over near the Big Horn?'

'Of course. What of them?'

'Cattle bin stolen, an' one of Ben Hardacre's riders killed.'

'So I heard.' Jim knew what was coming, but stayed cool.

'So how come you ain't getting hit?'

Jim shook his head, his eyes boring into Sheriff Todd's. The sheriff made no move to intervene.

Jim turned to the bartender. 'Couple of cool beers please, Sid.' He turned back to face Ed. The sheriff was nowhere to be seen, but three of Ed's riders were now standing menacingly near, plus Red West and a cowboy Jim hadn't seen before. The stranger fingered a brace of pearl-handled Colts menacingly.

'You gonna answer my question?' Ed Howes spat out the words, his finger pointing at Jim.

'Who's this feller?' Jim Jackson demanded, gesturing towards the stranger.

Ed looked across at the cowboy. 'He

works for Alexander.'

'Brown's man, eh?'

'Never mind him. Answer my question.' The pitch of Ed's voice moved up a tone with each utterance.

Billy spoke. 'Let it go, uncle.'

Jim patted Billy's arm, and took a sip of his beer, feeling Billy's presence at his elbow. 'How come *your* spread hasn't been hit?' Jim asked Ed.

Ed's face grew even sterner. 'My spread?' he repeated indignantly. 'Injuns are too scared to raid my spread.' He poked a finger into Jim's chest.

The sound of a couple of chairs scraping on the floorboards filled the bar, their occupiers sensing trouble, making sure to be out of the firing line.

The hairs on Jim's skin came to attention, every instinct shouting at him to lash out, but the reactions of his youth had long since passed; he resisted the temptation to move his hand towards his side-iron.

'Ed, me and Billy came in to have a quiet cool drink. Let's not start something we might both regret.'

Instead of having a calming effect, Ed's face turned redder. His finger prodded Jim's chest again. 'I'll answer my question for you. Your spread ain't been hit because of that squaw woman you got livin' with you.'

Jim's huge fist smashed into Ed's bulbous nose. Blood spurted wildly, but before Jim could follow up, a shaved-down wagon-wheel spoke wielded by the bartender crashed onto the back of his head. His body slumped to the beer-stained floor. Fist raised, Billy rushed forward a split second before a heavy slug buried itself deep in his gut. The bullet propelled Billy backwards, his flailing body smashing a card table as the force of the slug sent him on his way to the bar room floor.

Blood flooded the front of Billy's shirt; his green eyes were wide with shock. 'I bin sh . . . shot,' was all he said before blackness filled his dying eyes.

The thin gunman holstered his six-gun. 'Fetch the doc,' the Lafayette

Kid shouted to no one in particular.

Then he laid into Jim's prone figure with both feet. Ed Howe was too shocked to say a word. He leaned against the bar for support, wiping his face and neck with a red-spotted neckerchief; he hadn't expected what had just happened.

'That's enough,' the bartender shouted. The Kid turned to the bartender. 'Gimme another bottle, and . . . ' He grabbed the front of the bartender's shirt, pulling the terrified man towards him. He stuck his six-gun under the bartender's nose and added, 'Don't ever tell me what to do, savvy?' The Kid was grinning, but there was no humour in his words.

The click of the gun being cocked echoed around the saloon. The bartender looked as if he was about to wet his pants; his face was redder than a ripe strawberry and sweat poured from his pores. He nodded, too scared to speak.

The gunman released the hammer on

his Colt and holstered the weapon with a flourish, then turned to see what the scuffling noises behind him were. Two men were dragging Jim Jackson's unconscious body through the swing door, dumping it on the boardwalk. The Kid poured out two whiskies. 'Brown'll be pleased with that,' he said to Red West. Then both men toasted each other.

The men returned then and dragged out Billy's body, leaving a trail of blood across the well-worn wooden floor-boards.

Ed Howes motioned to his three cowboys, and they left.

Jim Jackson was eventually taken over to Doctor Hollis for treatment; Billy's body was taken to the undertaker.

16

Three Pines Fork

Jeff Jackson was a contented man; he felt like singing. The first consignment of mustangs — the proceeds of six weeks' hard toil — had been caught, corralled, and the best ones saddle-broken; he knew the army would be delighted with the quality.

The sun was warm on his face as he headed Atlas north-west, Clem and Dan flanking him, equally pleased with themselves. The five-day drive to Fort Ellis was finally happening.

Clem looked across at his brother and cousin, unable to hold in his happiness. 'We're on our way. We're on our way.'

Dan smiled back. 'Sure are, cuz,' he said as Mike French rode up.

Ten miles after they had left the banks of the Boulder River a single gunshot rang out, the sound echoing around the low hills surrounding the lush valley. The bullet smacked into a rock, ricocheting into the undergrowth. The four riders turned as a second shot rang out.

Jeff slumped from Atlas's back, his body hitting the brown earth with a deep thud.

'No!' Clem yelled, as simultaneously Mike shouted to take cover.

Dan made a grab for Atlas's reins. The skittish horse, spooked by the gunfire, shied first one way then the other. Finally, Dan caught the animal's reins and spurred his own horse behind a cluster of rocks, dragging a reluctant Atlas behind him. Mike and Clem tugged their rifles free and vaulted from their saddles, slapping the rumps of their horses as another shot rang out loudly; this time the bullet kicked up dust a couple of feet from Clem's boot. The two riderless horses followed Dan behind the rocks as Clem and Mike manhandled Jeff to cover.

Jeff groaned and cursed profanely as blood oozed from a wound high up on his right thigh. Clem tore away his bandanna and tied it around the top of Jeff's thigh, placing a strong stick into the loop of the red material to make a tourniquet. Clem was relieved his brother was not dead; the way Jeff's body had dropped to the ground had made him fear the worst.

Another couple of shots rang out. Mike whispered, 'Shooter's up on that hill, behind them rocks. Might be two of 'em.'

Clem peered over the top of the boulder, seeing a small puff of smoke rise from where Mike had indicated.

'Must be using long rifles,' Mike opined. 'That's way out of range for my Winchester.'

'Pity we don't have Billy's Sharps with us,' Clem said.

'What's happened to Jeff?' Dan called out from behind the boulder he was using for cover.

'Thigh wound,' Mike called back,

weighing up the alternatives. 'Dan, when I shout, put a few shots at that stand of rocks on the ridge. Aim for the big blue-grey rock to the left of that fir tree. Can you see it?'

The sound of Dan's boot scraping for a hold on the rock was the only thing to break the silence. Once in position, Dan called out, 'I see it, but that's still too far for my Winchester.'

'Just do it,' Mike ordered. 'Them bushwhackers don't know you only have a Winchester. Fire every few seconds to distract whoever it is up there. I'm gonna work my way around to come up behind the bushwhacking sons-of-bitches. OK?'

'You got it. Here goes.' Dan levered a round into the chamber of his newly acquired Winchester and fired off three shots in quick succession. As predicted, the bullets fell short, but ricocheted from the rocks with a whine.

Mike ran across behind Dan and the horses, keeping the rocks between him and the shooters, his pounding heart in his mouth. Every couple of seconds a bullet from Dan's Winchester smacked into a rock below the spot where Mike was headed. No answering shot was heard.

Dan stopped firing when the eleven shots had emptied his Winchester. He was reloading when Mike's shout drifted across the ground. Dan looked over the cold grey boulder. Mike was standing on a rock waving his hat.

'Looks like it's all clear,' Dan told Clem. 'I'll go take a look. You wait there with Jeff.'

Dan jumped up onto his horse and rode to the base of the rock formation.

Mike was climbing down. 'Shooters have gone,' he pronounced. 'I caught a glimpse of them as they breasted that ridge; three of 'em. One rode a tall black; another rode a pinto; one was wearing a sheepskin.' He held out four expended big-calibre cartridges. 'Found these,' he said. 'From their tracks I'd say one of the horses had a dropped shoe on its right foreleg.

Should be easy to identify.' Dan nodded his understanding. 'How's Jeff?' Mike asked.

He climbed up into his saddle. 'Jump up, we'll go find out,' he said.

Clem had got Jeff onto his unsteady feet and was trying to keep Atlas reasonably still. Jeff made a grab for the saddle pommel and grimaced when he placed his left foot into the stirrup. Mike sprang down from behind Dan and took hold of Jeff. Once the wounded man's foot was in place the rest, although intensely painful, was easy.

'You sure you can ride?'

Jeff nodded, his screwed-up eyes telling the real story.

* * *

Jeff flinched, suppressing the inward scream as he bit down hard on the leather belt between his teeth. The searing hot knife burned into the flesh on the outside of his left thigh; Jeff almost passed out from the intense pain.

'That's got 'er,' Doctor Hollis grunted. 'You'll live. I guess,' he added with a grin.

* * *

'Kid, you'd better lay low for a while.' Alexander Brown pulled open the top drawer of his desk, handing the Kid a wad of notes. 'Here's two hundred. More than enough to stake you to a good time.'

The Kid's grey eyes narrowed. 'When do I get the rest?'

'Soon,' Brown soothed. 'Soon as I've sold the herd.'

The Kid was not completely satisfied with Brown's assurances. 'What about my share of the silver?'

Brown had to fight hard to keep control of his exasperation. 'Heck, Kid. It'll take months before we can see any profit from that venture. You'll have to be patient.'

There was a great deal of menace in the Kid's frown. Brown put an arm around his shoulder. 'Kid,' he purred, 'you know you can trust me. Hmm? I'll get some more money to you in a week or so. Just let me know where and I'll do the rest.' He smiled. 'I won't let you down.'

The Lafayette Kid shrugged away Brown's avuncular arm. 'Better not!' he snorted. 'Remember, I know everything.' He grinned sinisterly. 'In any case, let me down an' I'll kill you.'

Alexander Brown's spine chilled; he knew this was no empty threat.

'Have you decided where you will go?' he asked.

The Kid pondered a moment. 'Virginia City.'

Brown nodded. 'Virginia City it is. I'll send the money to the Cattleman's Bank there. What's your real name?' Brown asked. 'Can't call yourself the Lafayette Kid. Draw to much attention to yourself.'

The Kid scowled through jaundiced

eyes, not wishing to reveal his true identity, but the realization that he wouldn't get his money if he didn't finally dawned on him.

'Potts,' he said curtly. 'Mr P. Potts.'

Without thinking, Brown asked, 'What's the P stand for?'

The Kid answered instinctively, 'Percival.'

Brown declined to repeat the full name out loud, figuring the Kid might not approve. *Percy Potts*, he thought, not as scary as his alias.

The Lafayette Kid departed at first light, leaving Alexander Brown with a dilemma; the Kid was a loose end that needed tidying up one way or another. After giving the matter considerable thought he decided to allow the Kid's destination to be known.

But the Kid didn't stay long in Virginia City. In the two days he was there he got to thinking: he didn't trust Brown one iota. He decided to head back to White Bluff, figuring to think things through in the saloon.

Brown's foreman, Red West, was there with a couple of the ranch hands. Red and the Kid settled down with a bottle.

17

The funeral of Billy Welch was a sombre affair. Billy's lifeless body lay in a pine coffin by a stand of cottonwoods near the creek. Uncle Jim hadn't recovered sufficiently to attend.

Dan — being Billy's closest relative there — was visibly the most upset, and struggled manfully to read a short eulogy he had composed himself.

At the subsequent inquest, Circuit Judge Gains had delivered a verdict of unlawful killing, saying the case would remain open until the perpetrator was taken into custody.

Word was that the Lafayette Kid hadn't been seen since the day he shot Billy. Sheriff Todd had appeared to go through the motions, taken statements, let it be known he had visited the Circle B ranch and had spoken at length to Alexander Brown, who now claimed the

Kid had never been on his payroll. Todd tried to make out that the killer was unknown to him. Subsequently changing his story, the sheriff said he'd heard a rumour that the Lafayette Kid had been seen in Virginia City.

Sanchez rode in, saying the Kid was in White Bluff.

As soon as he heard this, Mike French saddled up.

Clem watched the cloud of dust. 'Where's Mike going?' he asked Dan.

'Said he had some urgent business to attend to.'

'Where?'

'Didn't say.' Dan rubbed his chin. 'All I know is that he was mighty agitated.'

18

White Bluff

The batwing doors swung shut with a screeching crash, heralding the tall stranger's entrance. Mike French peered around the dark saloon, his right hand hovering near the Colt on his hip. In one corner four men were playing cards. A couple of soiled doves hung around looking for business. Five or six cowboys stood at the bar. One of the girls moved towards the newcomer, but stopped abruptly when she noticed his expression. All but two of the men at the bar turned their heads, stiffening visibly before edging away.

The two men who didn't move were watching their own and the newcomer's reflection in the large mirror hanging behind the bar. One, Mike recognized as Red West; the other was dressed in black, fresh dust on his long coat and boots testifying to his recent arrival.

Straggling lanks of dirty-blond hair spilled from under his dusty black hat across his collar.

'I'm looking for the Lafayette Kid.' Mike's challenging words echoed around the barroom.

A giggling saloon girl appeared at the top of the stairs, a fresh-faced cowboy on her arm. She quickly took in the situation and her hand went to her mouth. The pair retraced their steps, recognizing the need to stay clear of the developing tension below.

Mike took a couple of steps forward. He knew what his quarry looked like; only one man fitted the bill. The presence of the white-tailed palomino with one dropped shoe tethered to the hitching rail outside confirmed its owner was inside.

Red West slid a couple of paces along the bar. Still, the man in black didn't turn around. The other drinkers crowded against the far wall.

'I said, I am looking for the Lafayette Kid,' Mike repeated. Still no one

223

answered. 'You,' Mike called out to the black-clad figure, 'at the bar.' He pointed a finger. 'You he?'

Slowly, the man turned his head, his cold grey eyes taking in the measure of the challenger, a sneer of defiance on his face. A tiny muscle at the corner of his mouth twitched, but otherwise he showed no emotion. He raised the shot-glass he was holding in his right hand and tossed the whiskey into his mouth. Grinning sickeningly, but saying nothing, he turned back to face the mirror. The bartender slipped away to the far end of the counter.

'Hey. Barkeep!' the Kid yelled. 'Where d'ya think you're goin'?' The barman froze. 'More whiskey!' he yelled. The barman was rooted to the spot. 'Now!' The Kid banged the counter with his glass.

Hesitantly the barman shuffled forward; his hand shook wildly as he picked up a bottle. He filled the Kid's glass. Red West had turned side-on to the bar.

'Don't spill it!' the Kid ordered. 'Leave the bottle.' Satisfied with the barman's efforts, the Kid raised the glass to his lips and took a noisy sip. 'What'd you say, Bub?' the Kid said to Mike's reflection.

Mike was ready for anything. 'You the Lafayette Kid?' Mike issued his challenge.

'Might be.' The Kid sneered into the mirror between sips. 'But ain't.' He grinned. The Kid slowly turned his body side ways-on to the challenger. 'Anyway. Who wants to know?'

Mike eyed his quarry coldly, every sinew tightening. He said nothing.

'Hmm?' the Kid mewed. 'Cat got yer tongue?'

Red sniggered.

Mike wasn't fazed by the show of bravado; he knew the Kid was playing to the gallery. He said coolly, 'I'm asking you for the last time. Are you the Lafayette Kid?'

In one blurred movement of his left hand the Kid snatched up the half-full shot-glass and hurled it at Mike, simultaneously going for his gun with his right.

The Kid was lightning-fast. The pearl-handled Colt bucked in his hand; a terrifying sneer filled his mad-dog eyes, which suddenly began to glaze as the force of Mike's bullet tore though his chest muscles and into his heart.

The Lafayette Kid reeled backwards several steps before crumpling to the sawdust-covered floor of the saloon. Red West was slower; his lifeless body slammed back against the bar before his gun cleared its holster, a bloody hole in his chest where Mike's second bullet had hit him.

Wisps of blue smoke hung in the air. The stench and taste of burnt powder in his nostrils and mouth, Mike French holstered his gun and looked down at the two dead men slumped against the bar. 'That's for Billy Welch.' He grimaced, knowing it had been murder. Vengeance was what he called it. He had never for one moment considered an alternative ending once he had learned the name of Billy's killer; there would have been no pleasure in that. And in any case, after a lengthy trial there was even a chance that the Kid would have walked free if Alexander Brown had bought the jury. Even if the Kid had been found guilty of killing Billy someone else would have had the pleasure of stretching his neck.

Outside, heavy footfalls pounded the boardwalk. The saloon doors swung open. Sheriff Todd stepped into the saloon; he pointed a shotgun at Mike.

Mike looked deep into the sheriff's eyes. 'They went for their guns,' he said dispassionately, looking around for support. 'Self-defence?' he called out questioningly.

One man nodded, but another shouted, 'No way, sheriff. He' — he pointed at Mike French — 'gunned them down in cold blood.'

Mike swivelled to face his accuser, but before he could utter a word, the barrel of the shotgun smashed down onto the back of Mike's head.

Sheriff Todd turned over Mike's body, handcuffing his hands behind him. 'Get 'im up,' he ordered his deputy. 'Let's get him locked up.'

The deputy called Mike's accuser to help, and the two men dragged Mike's unconscious body out of the saloon.

Sheriff Todd noticed the trail of crimson liquid mixing with the straw-coloured sawdust. So the gunman had taken a bullet.

The deputy locked the cell door; blood was spreading across Mike's shirt. 'Shall I fetch the doc?' he asked.

Sheriff Todd nodded.

Sheriff Todd couldn't believe his luck; this would raise his worth even higher in Alexander Brown's eyes. He sent a note to Brown informing him that the Lafayette Kid and Red West had been shot and killed by Mike French, and that he had French under lock and key.

Alexander Brown was as pleased with the news as Sheriff Todd had hoped. He rode to town immediately.

'Here's a chance to get rid of one of them Double-J bastards,' Brown said. 'Let's make certain sure everyone knows you have the son-of-a-bitch locked up.'

★ ★ ★

'Another round of drinks,' shouted Alexander Brown. He patted Sheriff Todd on the shoulder. 'Drink up, boys. A toast to the man who captured Red's killer.'

'Sheriff Todd!' the drinkers chorused. Brown had been buying whiskey all afternoon.

Brown raised his glass again. 'To the memory of Red West. Best ramrod I ever had. You all knew him.'

Heads nodded. 'Red West!' Another chorus of cheers.

'Too young to die,' Brown added sombrely. 'Hanging's too good for the low-down skunk that killed him.'

The drunken rabble was well on the

way to anarchy, but Brown knew he would have to dig a lot deeper before they were drunk enough to become a lynch party.

Lars Andersen had heard enough; he left by the back door.

'And don't stop till you get there,' Andersen instructed the stableboy. 'Make sure you put this note in Dan or Clem's hand. Got it?' The boy nodded. 'Here's a quarter.'

The boy pushed the coin into his pocket along with the note and sped off down the street. The stableboy met Dan and Clem on the road; they had Jeff in the buckboard, taking him to see Laurie and Doctor Hollis, their horses trailing along behind. All three were in good spirits until they read the note.

'You go on ahead,' Jeff encouraged. 'I can manage the buckboard. Get Mike out.'

Dan and Clem spurred away in company with the stableboy. Jeff whipped up the horses and followed.

The alley at the side of the jail was

deep in shadow as Dan and Clem dismounted and tethered their mounts. Dan peered through a window. Sheriff Todd was sitting at his desk going over some papers, a thin cigarette dangling from his lips. Smoke curled up into his eyes as he turned to face the knock at the door. He looked up and grinned: he was expecting a lynch party; they were early.

'It ain't locked,' he called out a split second before the door burst open. The cigarette fell from his open mouth, his eyes widening when he saw the two six-guns drawing a bead on him. The metallic sound of hammers being cocked caused him to swallow nervously. Todd's bladder threatened to spill its contents down his leg.

'Don't do anything stupid, boys,' he stammered out.

'Open the cell,' the taller of the two men ordered. The other man moved around the desk and removed the sheriff's gun from its holster.

Sheriff Todd lifted a large bunch of

keys from a nail on the wall behind him. 'Easy, boys.' His hands trembled; the keys jangled loudly as he got up to obey the order. The iron-barred door swung back with a creak.

Dan peered into the gloom. 'Bring that lantern.' He saw Mike was unconscious. 'Get inside,' he ordered Todd. 'Help him up.'

Clem unlocked the side door leading to the alley and took a peek outside, seeing Jeff pull up the buckboard.

He whispered, 'Buckboard's here.'

Dan took the weight of Mike's almost limp body from the sheriff and half-dragged Mike out into the alley and into the buckboard. 'Get going, Jeff.'

Jeff shook out the reins and headed the buckboard back to the Double-J.

'Get back in the cell,' Clem ordered. 'Drop your gunbelt.' Todd did as he was told; he was no hero. 'Kick it over here.' Using his foot Clem slid the gunbelt to one side. 'Turn around. Face the wall.' Sheriff Todd turned away.

The heavy Colt smashed down and Ethan Todd collapsed in a heap. Clem pushed the sheriff's prone body into the cell and locked the door. He then locked the front door and pulled down the shades on both windows. Locking the side door he swung himself into the saddle, a wave of elation sweeping through him like a bolt of lightning.

Dan was waiting on his horse. 'Let's go, cousin.' The pair sped away into the night.

*   *   *

Alexander Brown felt that the time had arrived. 'Red's murderer's sitting in our jail. Eating our food. Drinking our coffee,' he called out. 'And what did he do to deserve this? Nothing! Should be hung.' His acting was first class. 'Why, if I was a young man, I'd get me a rope . . . ' He allowed his words of incitement to trail away.

'Somebody get a rope,' one man shouted.

'Yeah, let's string him up,' another called out.

Lanterns and torches lit the grim faces of the lynch mob as they marched towards the jail.

19

White Bluff

Heads turned towards the thunderous sound of massed horses approaching. A dense dust cloud on the trail into town rose thick and dark above the roofs of the buildings. Around the corner of the livery stable came a neat column of twos, resplendent in blue and yellow; the Union flag flanked by a guidon fluttered stiffly behind the straight-backed officer leading the troop.

The officer held up a hand to halt his men. 'Sergeant. Dismount and rest the men.' The young officer stepped down from his horse. 'Gentlemen.' He addressed the group of men who had come out into the street. 'Lieutenant Marcus Hart, B Troop, 3rd Cavalry.' He saluted. 'Where can I find Doctor Hollis?'

The doctor stepped forward. 'I'm Hollis.'

The officer saluted. 'Our presence in White Bluff is explained in this letter.'

Doctor Hollis took the document and read the contents.

'As you have read, sir, I have orders from the governor to establish law and order in White Bluff, whilst a number of serious allegations that have been made regarding the town sheriff and a prominent local rancher, name of Alexander Brown, are investigated.'

Two of Brown's men, lounging outside the saloon, heard the lieutenant's words and made a dash for their horses.

Lieutenant Hart coughed and carried on with his explanation. 'Yours was not the only letter received by the governor. Some weeks ago a citizen named Walter Schultz wrote a letter setting out the situation here in White Bluff, describing in some detail a number of alarming and unlawful instances, including three killings within the town boundary — one, a ranch hand working for him. He alleged that the town sheriff was oblivious of his duty, citing instances of criminal damage to buildings, attacks on persons and property, plus cattle-rustling. Obviously the governor was concerned. Hence our presence.'

Doctor Hollis clenched his teeth and nodded.

'I would be obliged if you would tell me where I can find Mr Schultz? I should like to speak with him.'

'Nobody's seen him for some time.'

'He's missing?'

'Sure is. And his son's dead. Killed in a gunfight, so he can't help.'

Lieutenant Hart slapped his gauntlet against his thigh. 'Please direct me to the sheriff's office.'

'It's down the end of the street,' called out another man, 'but he ain't there. He left early. Went to the Circle B to raise a posse. That's Brown's place. Then he's going after a feller named Mike French, out at the Double-J.'

'Doctor,' the lieutenant said through gritted teeth, 'by the authority bestowed on me by the governor, I am declaring a state of martial law until the US Marshal gets here.' The lieutenant held up a hand to halt the doctor. He turned. 'Sergeant Brettell, take the first squad and secure the town. Doctor, I'd be obliged to receive directions to the Double-J.'

'I'll come with you. Jack, fetch my horse, will you?'

Minutes later Lieutenant Hart led the rest of his troop out of town.

20

Double-J ranch

The sound of horsemen approaching was clear in the otherwise quiet terrain; every man knew exactly who it was and why they were coming. Clem positioned himself at the side of the ranch house. Jeff sat on a rocking chair on the shady front porch, cradling a Winchester across his knees.

Dan stood in the open doorway of the ranch house. 'I make it seven or eight riders, coming slow and easy,' he said.

The first of the horses came into view through the fir trees around the side of the bluff, one or two whinnying nervously, sensing danger. There were eight riders, all now clearly visible through the dusty haze, moving at a steady canter, slowing to a walk as they neared the ranch house.

The leader pushed his horse ahead of the others; the star pinned to the front of his coat glinted in the sunlight. A bloodstained bandage showed clearly under his hat. He held up a hand, signalling the riders to halt.

Sheriff Todd had carefully rehearsed what he wanted to say before he had left his office, and again, many times on the journey to the Double-J ranch, but now he faced the men he sought, his lips dried, his tongue seemed to swell up to fill his mouth. At that moment all eyes were upon him, recognizing that here in this pressure cooker of a situation the centre of attention had got himself tongue-tied.

The sheriff coughed loudly to clear his throat, and spat, nervous tension eating away at his insides. On paper all had seemed simple: go in, announce he had come to rearrest the escapee and arrest the men who had helped him escape. Actually that was the last thing the sheriff wanted. He was counting on these men to resist arrest so that he had an excuse to shoot the lot of them, just as Alexander Brown had ordered. He ran through the words again in his head, but still hesitated.

He had more than enough men to back him up. The three snipers he had put in position would fix the two Jackson boys. Brown's gunslicks would handle the rest.

The sound of a second group of horses filled the air, coming at a gallop, the telltale jingle of equipment confirming who they were. Jeff knew the sound well — US Cavalry. All eyes turned to look. The troop of blue-coated horsemen halted in a shower of dust.

'Sheriff!' Lieutenant Hart shouted.

Sheriff Todd suddenly found his voice. Ignoring the cavalryman he called out, 'I call upon you to surrender Mike French to me. Hand him over.'

None of the Double-J men answered.

Lieutenant Hart called out again. 'Sheriff. You and your men will surrender your weapons to me, now!'

Alexander Brown's voice boomed

out. 'Lieutenant! Get your men out of here. This is not your business.'

At that moment Jim's dog rushed into the yard, barking its head off. It sprang at the nearest horse. The horse skittered and reared; one of Brown's cowboys drew his pistol and fired, missing the dog by a mile. Everything now seemed to move into slow motion.

Whitey Bell's bullet smacked into the wall of the ranch house near to Clem's head. Ray Cole went for his Colt as his horse reared, and was shot through the head by Dan. Jeff raised his Winchester but didn't fire. Clem walked out into the yard and drew his Remington.

All over the yard horses were rearing, whinnying, and skittering. Dust flew, polluting the air; nobody could get a clear shot. As the first bullets began to fly Sheriff Todd was pitched to the ground. Whitey Bell, a smoking pistol in his hand, spurred his mount forward, aiming his horse at Clem, who dived out of the way. Whitey dragged on the reins and his horse skidded to a halt.

He took deadly aim at Clem, but before he could squeeze the trigger the deafening crack of a Winchester put a bullet through him, the spent projectile passing right through Whitey's body to lodge itself in Alexander Brown's throat.

Brown's cowboys continued to fire at the Double-J men, who returned their fire with deadly consequences.

The snipers on the ridge squeezed off a couple of shots, but, seeing the negative way things were going, mounted their horses and galloped away.

When the dust settled, a calm serenity came over the ranch yard.

'Sergeant, see to those men,' Lieutenant Hart ordered, pointing to the prone bodies.

One cavalryman had taken a bullet, but was not wounded seriously. Clem nursed a blood-soaked arm. Dan and Sanchez picked themselves up from where they had dived for cover.

From inside the ranch house a gruff voice shouted repeatedly, demanding to know what was happening. No one answered Jim Jackson's cries for information as he lay in his darkened bedroom, still too weak to stand.

'You OK?' Dan asked Clem.

'I'll live,' Clem answered wryly.

One horse was squealing like a banshee. A single shot rang out, putting the animal out of its misery.

Jeff limped down the ranch-house steps using the Winchester for support; the wound in his leg had started bleeding again.

Lieutenant Hart dismounted, handed his reins to a trooper. He took off his hat and wiped the dust and sweat from his eyes. 'I sure as hell wasn't expecting this carnage.'

Sergeant Gomez called out, 'Sir.' Hart turned. 'Four dead, one wounded in the throat; looks pretty serious, might not make it. The doctor's seeing what he can do. Sheriff's out cold, but he'll live.'

Lieutenant Hart nodded. 'See if there's a wagon around, put the bodies in that. We'll take them back to town.'

'Wagon's under the lean-to at the back of the barn,' Jeff stated.

Sergeant Gomez took two men and went to organize the makeshift hearse.

Lieutenant Hart turned to Jeff, explaining why he was there.

Jeff nodded.

Dan looked up from the task of tying a strip of cloth around Clem's arm, pronouncing that the wound looked clean and wouldn't need amputating. His crude attempt at black humour drew grins, but no laughs.

The corpses were laid out in a line by a squad of troopers. Jeff felt no emotion as he examined the contorted faces, except a tinge of sadness for the cowboys that had died thinking they were members of a legitimate posse; they had paid for that with their lives.

Nearby, Alexander Brown coughed up blood. Doc Hollis dabbed at the blood pulsing through the bandanna Sergeant Gomez had tied around Brown's neck as a makeshift bandage.

Jeff took off his coat and spread it over Brown to keep him warm. Brown's face was streaked with anguish and pain. He tried to speak but couldn't. The doctor shook his head.

Sheriff Todd started to come round. His right leg was broken where a horse had stomped him and he groaned with pain as he regained consciousness.

Jeff bent over the sheriff and plucked the tin star from his shirt, tearing the material in the process. 'You ain't fit to wear that,' he said.

Todd stared into Jeff's eyes, but found no words, rehearsed or otherwise.

Horses hitched, Sergeant Gomez drove the wagon into the yard. The corpses were lifted in and made secure. Then Alexander Brown and the sheriff were carried to the wagon and put inside. Brown was delirious, mumbling unintelligible ramblings and ravings; blood spilled down his chin each time his mouth opened.

Lieutenant Hart requested that all

accompany him and his men into White Bluff, to enable statements to be taken; he could send a rider with his report to Fort Ellis.

★　★　★

Laurie Andersen was waiting for news, praying for Jeff's safe deliverance. It had taken all her father's parental control to keep her from saddling up and heading out to the Double-J.

She ran to the line of horsemen, not seeing Jeff amongst them, and thinking the worst. The troop of cavalry passed by; Lieutenant Hart saluted and offered a polite greeting. Laurie ignored the gesture as she searched the tired faces: Dan, Clem, his arm held across his chest in a bloodstained sling, the wagon driven by a solemn-faced trooper alongside Sergeant Gomez. There was no sign of Jeff Jackson. Tears welled in her eyes to run down her face, which showed all the signs of the hurt she felt inside. She climbed the step to the boardwalk and leaned on her father, who had appeared from the store. He held her tightly.

The exhausted column halted in front of the doctor's house, where feverish activity suddenly commenced.

Laurie watched as the doctor climbed into the rear of the wagon to organize the removal of the bodies; two other men followed him. She recognized Sheriff Todd, who cursed at the men carrying him, demanding they take care. Laurie couldn't bear to look, but at the same time could not keep away. She moved slowly to the wagon.

The canvas cover was thrown back, exposing a number of bloodstained bodies. Doc was bending over one body. Laurie couldn't see the face; couldn't see who it was. All she could make out was the blood-red bandanna around his neck. Then she recognized the coat covering the body — Jeff's coat.

Doctor Hollis turned away. 'He's dead,' was all he said.

The words ripped the heart from Laurie's breast and she fainted. Lars Andersen caught his daughter before she could fall.

Lars shouted, 'Who's that?'

'Alexander Brown,' replied the doctor solemnly.

Lars held on tightly to his daughter. 'Not Jeff?' he challenged.

'Heck no!' said the doctor. 'It's Brown.'

Lars laid Laurie's body onto the boardwalk and accepted a canteen of water someone offered him. He poured some on his hand and splashed the cool liquid onto his daughter's face.

'Laurie,' he said soothingly. 'Laurie.'

Her eyes flickered open. Her hand reached for her forehead. She looked into her father's flint-grey eyes.

'Laurie,' he repeated, 'it's not Jeff.'

Laurie stared at her father in a trance of disbelief. 'N-not Jeff?' The words were at odds with the look in her eyes.

'No.' Lars helped his daughter

struggle unsteadily to her feet, her head turning constantly this way and that. Uncontrollable tears of relief ran down her cheeks. It was a while before she was able to say anything else.

Clem saw her and rode wearily over.

'Wh-where's Jeff?' Laurie sobbed.

Clem looked vacantly at her; he hadn't heard her question. He shook his head.

'Where's Jeff?' she shouted. This time Clem heard.

His saddle creaked as he turned to look back the way they had come. 'He's following.' Clem pointed.

Heart pounding, Laurie ran towards the dust and heat haze. A buckboard came into view. She looked longingly at the raised arm, her tears almost obscuring her vision. She waved back then set off running again, covering the ground between her and her lover in no time.

Almost out of breath, one hand at her throat, the other clutching a tear-stained handkerchief, she reached out, steeling herself against fainting. 'Jeff,' she gasped.

Jeff halted the horses, motioning for her to climb up next to him. Their arms entwined around each other, their lips saying all that needed to be said.

THE END

We do hope that you have enjoyed reading this large print book.

Did you know that all of our titles are available for purchase?

We publish a wide range of high quality large print books including:
Romances, Mysteries, Classics
General Fiction
Non Fiction and Westerns

Special interest titles available in large print are:
The Little Oxford Dictionary
Music Book, Song Book
Hymn Book, Service Book

Also available from us courtesy of Oxford University Press:
Young Readers' Dictionary
(large print edition)
Young Readers' Thesaurus
(large print edition)

For further information or a free brochure, please contact us at:
Ulverscroft Large Print Books Ltd.,
The Green, Bradgate Road, Anstey,
Leicester, LE7 7FU, England.
Tel: (00 44) **0116 236 4325**
Fax: (00 44) **0116 234 0205**

THE HOT SPURS

Boyd Cassidy

When the riders of the Bar 10 run up against an escaped prisoner and his ruthless gang, they find themselves in deep trouble. Bret Jarvis and his henchmen are heading to Mexico, where men of the Circle J ranch have returned from a profitable cattle drive — making them sitting targets for a raid. But Gene Adams and his Bar 10 cowboys are soon in hot pursuit — all they need to do is stop the outlaws before they reach the border . . .

LONG RIDIN' MAN

Jake Douglas

They call him 'Hunter'. There is one man in particular for whom he searches: the man who destroyed his family. Trailing the killer, Hunter finds himself in a booming town short of one deputy sheriff: in need of cash, he pins on the badge. But the folk of Cimarron begin to wonder just who they've hired as their peacemaker. Once Hunter discovers why the town needed a fast gun so urgently, the odds are that it will be too late for him to get out alive . . .

POWDER RIVER

Jack Edwardes

As the State Governor's lawmen spread throughout Wyoming, the days of the bounty hunter are coming to a close. For hired gun Brad Thornton, this spells the end of an era. The men in badges aren't yet everywhere, though, and rancher Moreton Frewen needs immediate action: rustlers are stealing his stock, and Thornton is just the man to make the culprits pay. But these are no run-of-the-mill cattle thieves. The Morgan gang are ruthless killers, prepared to turn their hands to anything from bank robbery to murder . . .

THE HONOUR OF THE BADGE

Scott Connor

US Marshal Stewart Montague was a respected mentor to young Deputy Lincoln Hawk, guiding his first steps as a lawman and impressing upon him the importance of the honour of the badge. Twenty years later, the pair are pursuing a gang of bandits when Montague goes missing, presumed murdered. For six months, Hawk continues the mission alone, without success. But when he stumbles into the gang's hideout, there is a great shock in store. Seems his old companion isn't six feet under after all . . .

RETURN OF THE BANDIT

Roy Patterson

Villainous bounty hunter Hume Crawford is well-known for his brutal slayings: he will do anything to get his hands on those he seeks. Out to find and kill the legendary bandit Zococa, despite reports of the good-natured rogue's death, Crawford proceeds to shoot his way across the Mexican border. But he has attracted the attention of Marshal Hal Gunn and his deputy Toby Jones. As Crawford follows Zococa's trail, there are two Texas star riders on his . . .

THE PHANTOM STRIKES

Walt Keene

The desert terrain was once haunted by the Phantom — a blanched man on a pale-grey horse, who struck in the night and killed without mercy. Wild Bill Hickock shot the legend down once — and twenty years later, when the Phantom's son took up the torch, he did so again ... With both culprits dead, Hickock and his compadres are satisfied they have laid the ghost to rest. But when a mortally wounded man gasps that the spirit has returned, they must take up arms once more — against the Phantom's second son ...